THE ANGRY DARKNESS

In 1967 the war clouds were gathering again in the Middle East, and Kerim Soiron undertook his last mission as a British Military Intelligence Agent. After rescuing a lovely Arab dancer from a hospital in Cairo, Kerim was plunged into the pre-war intrigue that was rife in Damascus and Jerusalem. Then, a forced change of sides entailed another dangerous mission in Cairo. Finally, during the six-day war, he returned to besieged Jerusalem to stop a madman's crime directed against both Arabs and Jews.

CHARLES LEADER

THE ANGRY DARKNESS

Complete and Unabridged

LINFORD
Leicester

First published in Great Britain

First Linford Edition
published 1998

Copyright © 1968 by Charles Leader
All rights reserved

British Library CIP Data

Leader, Charles, *1938–*
    The angry darkness.—Large print ed.—
Linford mystery library
1. Detective and mystery stories
2. Large type books
I. Title
823.9′14 [F]

ISBN 0–7089–5344–1

Published by
F. A. Thorpe (Publishing) Ltd.
Anstey, Leicestershire
Set by Words & Graphics Ltd.
Anstey, Leicestershire
Printed and bound in Great Britain by
T. J. International Ltd., Padstow, Cornwall

This book is printed on acid-free paper

1

Escape From Egypt

The lights of Alexandria answered the twinkling of the stars, and the softly warm night breathed the mingling, cloying smells of the sea and the city. The square, menacing shape of the Quait Bai fortress moved slowly past on the port bow, a threatening silhouette against the darkness as the *Masara* cautiously detached herself from the remainder of the fishing fleet that lay festooned with nets in the shelter of the harbour. The quiet pulsing of her engine carried clearly across the oily black water, meeting the murmur of traffic and sound that came from Alexandria's streets. The two men who formed the crew of the *Masara* stood stiffly by the wheel, their dark faces silent and just a little tense. A group of Arabs in a passing boat called after them, and the man at the wheel hesitated a moment

1

before he answered the greeting. The fishing boat chugged slowly towards the harbour entrance, but there was no other challenge. The harbour bar drew back its protecting arms, and the *Masara*'s bows began to lift as she rode into the swelling waves. Before her lay the dark expanse of the Mediterranean.

Below decks Kerim Soiron felt the heavier movement of the open sea, and some of the bottled tension eased from his body. That period of silent waiting in the pitch darkness, unable to calculate either their progress or their chances had been the worst part of the whole operation. The job had been smooth and simple while he was handling it for himself, but this last stage had caused him to sweat. He was reasonably confident of the loyalty of the two fishermen on the deck above him, but he was not so certain of their capabilities if anything had gone wrong.

He straightened up from his crouching position, flexing his shoulders to ease the aching muscles across his back. He bumped his head upon the deckboards above and swore softly. Then he glanced to where the girl lay stretched out on the greasy bunk. He could not see her in the darkness, but her very stillness told him that she was still unconscious. Her breathing was so faint that he could not hear it above the low murmur of the engine and creaking timber. He hoped that she was still alive.

For a moment he wondered why Jackson had bothered to pull her out. He knew that she was Egyptian, a night club entertainer who danced under the stage name of Schererzade. He also knew that she was a British spy, and would shortly have been under sentence of death by the Egyptian authorities. He had removed her from a Cairo hospital while her doctors had considered her still unfit to be transferred to a security jail. Apart from that he knew very little. He remembered her sickly white face as they had manhandled her down through the tiny hatch into this cramped and smelly hole, and hoped again that they had not killed her. That would be too grim a joke.

The darkness was claustrophobic, made

nauseous by the reek of stale sweat, dead fish and oil fumes from the engine. Kerim hesitated a moment, feeling the pitching movement of the boat as she pushed into deeper seas, and then he groped for the steel ladder that gave exit. It was only a yard away and he pushed at the hatchway above as he started to climb. A hand drew the hatch open and he wriggled his head and shoulders out into the clean air. Two pairs of legs filled most of his view, and the two Arab faces looked down at him questioningly.

Kerim climbed up into the wheelhouse, breathing deeply. He said nothing, but looked back towards the lights of Alexandria. It was an unimpressive sky-line, broken only by the squat shape of the fortress guarding the harbour mouth. He was not sorry to be leaving Egypt again, and he exhaled and filled his lungs once more with the sharper sea air.

The two Arabs, brothers and joint owners of the *Masara*, smiled faintly. Kerim returned the smile but still nothing was said. The two fishermen had been friends from his youth, before

4

a charge similar to the one that faced the unconscious girl below had caused his exile from Egypt. He was not sure how much they knew about him now, or whether they would have cared. He was an old friend, and also this was a business proposition. The night's work had cost him plenty.

The *Masara* was now standing directly out to sea, rolling a little and creaking in her bones as she settled into a steady speed and course. White foam peeled off the black wavetops that gleamed under the bright starlight from the heavens. The smells of land had faded and Alexandria was just a thin necklace of yellow lights along the horizon. Kerim began to relax, and then the note of a more powerful engine sounded in the night. There was a sharp explanation from Hakim, the elder of the two Arabs, who gripped the wheel, and the boat lost a fractional amount of headway as his hands faltered. Kerim turned sharply.

He swore as he saw the fast approaching silhouette that sped towards them. Its engine swiftly became a roar, and as it

5

emerged from distance and darkness he recognized the sleek outline of a cruising patrol boat. The high steel bows were aimed straight towards them, as though the craft intended to slice the clumsy *Masara* cleanly in half. Already it was too late for Kerim to scramble below and so he crouched quickly below the open windows of the wheelhouse. His hand made a reflex move towards his jacket pocket where a .38 automatic hung heavily against his hip, but then he checked the action without drawing the gun clear. If the *Masara* was boarded then the game would be up, and resistance would only add extra bloodshed to the inevitable.

The patrol boat slowed as it turned past them, and the spot light in its bows illuminated a sweeping beam which swiftly settled on the *Masara*, raking her from stem to stern. Kerim wondered bitterly who had betrayed him, thinking of the two men and the girl who had helped him to pull off the rescue from the Cairo hospital, discarding them and then deciding that they must have been seen by some talkative Arab as they had loaded Schererzade aboard the fishing boat. Again his hand strayed towards the pocket that held his automatic, his mind deliberating on the romantic notion to sell his life dearly. A violent exit through a quick blaze of gunfire was perhaps preferable to arrest, identification, trial and subsequent execution. His hesitation was longer this time, but still he did not withdraw the automatic. It was still pointless.

The sound of the heavier engines died and a voice hailed them from across the sea. Kerim's understanding of Arabic was excellent, and he felt suddenly foolish as he recognized a simple greeting. He looked up and saw Hakim draw his tongue across his lips before he answered, and prayed that the Arab would not allow his nervousness to affect the tone of his reply. The fisherman's larynx moved jerkily, and then he answered. The words were hoarse and strained, but not enough to be noticeable across the intervening waves.

The spotlight went out, letting shadows

7

and darkness once more shroud the boat. The unseen voice aboard the patrol boat called a farewell '*Shalom*'. Peace be with you. And then the powerful engines roared again, drowning Hakim's relieved and echoing answer as she cruised off into the night.

As the engines faded Kerim stood up slowly. The faces of the two fishermen were still pale as they watched the large motor boat bearing away from them, and then Omar, the younger brother, broke the hushed silence.

'A routine patrol,' he said. 'They recognized the name of our boat. They think we are going fishing.'

Kerim nodded, swallowing hard and hoping that they had not noticed the fear he had felt when the patrol boat had stopped. Then Hakim said shortly:

'You should go back below. It is not safe while we are still so close to the shore. The police boat might come back.'

Kerim knew that having taken one close glance to identify them the patrol boat would not return, but he did not argue. He was a dangerous guest and he respected the wishes of his host. He descended through the hatchway once more, and steeled himself to suffer the smells and discomfort trapped within.

★ ★ ★

It was dawn when the *Masara* rendez-voused far out in the Mediterranean with the fishing boat that had been sent to meet them from Cyprus. The Cypriot craft was almost identical in shape, size and smell to the *Masara*, and Kerim picked out her outline on the horizon through his binoculars as the crimson sun began to spread fingering pathways of silver-red across the metallic sea. They were a little late, for the rendezvous should have been timed before the sun blinked its great red eye above the horizon, but the Cypriot still showed the two white lights that had been arranged as a signal from her mast. Kerim moved into the bows and flashed a torch twice as the *Masara* approached, thinking that it was all a bit too melodramatic and obvious now that the last shreds of darkness had disappeared. However, it was best to stick to his instructions.

The Cypriot was drifting, and Hakim carefully brought the *Masara* alongside, cutting his engines and allowing the two fishing boats to bump gently together in the low swell. The Cypriot had a crew of three and Kerim reached out a hand to help the man who quickly scrambled into the *Masara*. He was young, and although he wore a fisherman's clothes the smooth hand he extended had never hauled in a net. He said cheerfully:

'You must be Soiron. I'm Williamson, usually called Bill. I don't think we've met before.'

'We haven't.' Kerim smiled as he spoke, and pretended not to notice the dubious look that Williamson bestowed upon his own, smartly-styled grey suit. The young Englishman, for his Saxon grin could have no other origin, clearly expected mobile intelligence agents who skulked around in fishing boats to be suitably dressed for the part. Kerim could have explained that it would have

10

been difficult to stage what practically amounted to a kidnapping operation from a busy Cairo hospital in broad daylight dressed in a greasy jumper and seaboots, and that there had been no time since for him to change. However, that could come later, and the sad fact that nobody in the Mediterranean would ever mistake Williamson, usually called Bill, for anything but an Englishman dressed up in fisherman's clothing, he would tactfully refrain from mentioning at all.

As they shook hands Kerim said:

'The girl is down below. As the sun has got here before us we had best make the transfer as quickly as possible and then get away.'

Williamson nodded and they lost no time in bringing the unconscious Schererzade up on to the deck. They were helped by Omar while Hakim steadied the wheel, but even so it was a struggle to manoeuvre the girl's stretcher up through the tiny hatchway into the wheelhouse. She had been drugged before leaving Alexandria, and again Kerim was glad that he had taken this precaution to save her from any excess pain. It was much better that she should stay unconscious until they reached Cyprus.

The two fishing boats had drifted apart by the time the stretcher had been laid out upon the deck, and they had to wait while Hakim started the engine and brought them back alongside. The two hulls touched and rubbed together once more, creaking like contented mammals. Williamson returned to the second craft and one of the Cypriot crew came to help him. Kerim and Omar lifted the stretcher, waited until the two decks were momentarily level, and then passed it neatly into the hands waiting to receive it.

Kerim delayed to thank the two brothers, clasping hands briefly, and then he too went aboard the Cypriot. The two vessels parted and with a brief wave Hakim turned the *Masara* back towards Alexandria. The daylight was making him uneasy and he was in a hurry to be gone. Kerim watched their departure, and then felt the deck vibrate beneath his feet as the second engine started up. His new hosts were also anxious to return to their home port, and he turned to watch as their bows pointed north towards the island of Cyprus.

The stretcher still lay on the open deck. Schererzade was covered with a blanket and only her face was visible. It was a young face, aged with pain and worry, pale despite the dark Arab blood.

Williamson was standing beside her, looking dubious.

'Shall we get her below again?'

Kerim hesitated, and then knelt by the stretcher. He drew back the blanket and felt for her pulse. His eyes were still on her face, and something that might have been compassion stirred through him. She had been beautiful once, that much was obvious. He wondered if she would be again. Her pulse felt very weak against his fingertips, he could barely find it at all. He looked up into the concerned face of the young Englishman, and then shook his head.

'I don't think we should move her

13

anymore. She's already been moved about too much. I'm not sure of the extent of her injuries, but the nurse who helped me get her out of Cairo told me that too much movement might kill her.'

Williamson nodded, and then moved to speak to the Cypriot at the wheel. The fishing boat was well under way now, moving steadily through the calm blue seas as the sun brightened off her starboard quarter. The *Masara* had vanished from sight behind them. Kerim continued to kneel by the stretcher, and again he wondered why Jackson had taken the trouble to pull her out.

2

The Sunshine Island

Schererzade opened her eyes, struggling slowly through the dark mists of returning consciousness. The light above her seemed terribly far away and it took her a long time to reach it. At first there was just the feeling of dull pain, a strange disembodied aching with no other sensation of being alive. Only her eyelids moved, and after that her strength was drained. Above her was a smooth white ceiling, and her nostrils registered the familiar, antiseptic smell of a hospital.

She lay still, realizing that she was in a hospital bed, and the pattern of events that had brought her here began to crystallize into slow shape in her memory. The hurt in her body became more centralized, and she remembered the large black car that had deliberately run her down in one of the dingy back

15

streets of Cairo. Her hip and thigh had both been broken, and she suffered from a cracked pelvis. There had been several operations, she could not remember how many, and she looked for the bottle of blood plasma that normally dripped steadily through the thin rubber tube into her arm. She turned her head slowly, everything had to be done slowly, both thought and action, but the blood drip was not there. That meant that she must be getting better, but the new thought brought a new fear. The fear of being taken to an Egyptian jail. A shadow fell across her face and suddenly her heart was beating faster inside her breast.

She looked up, expecting to see the dark, glittering eyes of the Egyptian Major of security police who came to torment her waking moments. Instead, a pair of level grey eyes looked down into her own. The man standing beside her bed was neither taller nor heavier than the average European. He wore a grey suit, single breasted and neatly styled, with a white shirt and a slim blue tie. There was nothing outstanding about him and

16

his smile was friendly. His face showed a hint of dark blood which indicated that he was not wholly European, and yet she would have described him as handsome. It was a strangely ageless face, as though its owner had found no time to be young, and did not expect to grow old. That face had smiled down at her before, and the last of her memories began to merge into place. He had been wearing a white coat then, and had told her gently that her worries were almost over. She had been lifted and carried through long white corridors, and then a silent nurse had pricked a hypodermic syringe into her helpless arm. After that there had been nothing until now.

Kerim had seen the first frightened flicker of her eyes and said quietly:

'Don't be afraid. You are safe now. You are not in the hospital in Cairo any more. This is a British hospital in Nicosia, on the island of Cyprus.'

Schererzade lay still, her eyes wide and staring. She moved her lips and weakly formed the words:

'Who are you?'

'My name is Kerim Soiron.' He explained it carefully. 'A mutual friend of ours named Jackson gave me the job of getting you out of Egypt. I have some friends in Cairo who helped me, so it wasn't too difficult. We managed to acquire an ambulance by telephoning a fake distress call, and then taking the places of the regular drivers when they answered it. Then it was a simple matter of driving up to the hospital, walking inside and carrying you out. There wasn't even a special guard on your bed. The Egyptians knew you couldn't walk, and obviously they didn't regard you as important enough for anyone to try and rescue you. We did the job during the busiest part of the day and nobody seemed in the least suspicious. Once we were clear of the hospital we moved you from the ambulance to a private car and took you straight to Alexandria, and you and I sailed on a fishing boat that same night. One of my friends in Cairo was a trained nurse, she looked after you until we reached Alex, and then gave you some pain-killing drug to keep you unconscious throughout the rest of the journey. It was all very simple really.'

Schererzade had grasped little of the details, even though she had watched his face as he talked. She only understood that she was safe and that she could trust this man. It was an instinctive knowledge that came from inside her, and did not necessarily rest on his words. There was a certain part of her mind, independent of logic and reason, that could sense whether it was safe to trust or distrust any other person. She had never yet been wrong, and that peculiar intuition told her now that she could trust this stranger who had introduced himself as Kerim Soiron. The name was the only thing that had registered fully in her mind, and she said feebly:

'Kerim, that is an Arab name, but Soiron is not.'

Kerim smiled. 'Soiron was my father's name. He was French. He came to North Africa as a Sergeant in the French Foreign Legion. My mother was Egyptian, she gave me my Arab name.'

Schererzade closed her eyes for a

moment, the light was hurting them. Only her lips moved as she said:

'Kerim Soiron. It is a strange name.'

Kerim smiled, but he had noticed the closing of her eyes, and so had the young English nurse who had moved closer to the far side of the bed. Kerim knew what the nurse was about to say, and he nodded his understanding. He looked down again and said quietly:

'Goodbye, Schererzade. You are going to get well again, but right now you have no strength to waste on talking. I must go.'

Schererzade did not open her eyes, and after a moment he turned away, nodding briefly to the nurse as he left the small hospital ward. Schererzade lay without moving, and her fading thought was of the strange Arab-French name she had just heard. Kerim Soiron.

* * *

During the weeks that followed Kerim was quite content to stay and relax on the sunshine island of Cyprus. There was no urgent need for him to return to Beirut, which was the normal base of his operations, and he had heard no more from Jackson, the tough, sandy-haired Major of the Middle East department of British Military Intelligence who was his immediate superior. Williamson, usually called Bill, had pulled a few strings and found him a small apartment in Nicosia where he could stay at a nominal rent, and he was in no hurry to leave. He had learned that Williamson was a British Army Lieutenant seconded to Intelligence, but he had seen nothing of the young Englishman since the first few days following his arrival and assumed that he was absent on some dubious form of duty. Kerim was not displeased, for although he was grateful for the apartment he had no particular desire to see any more of British Intelligence or its minions. He was hopeful that they might forget him for a while.

Schererzade gradually became stronger, her mind was at rest and there was no longer the constant threat of an Egyptian jail which had psychologically delayed her recovery while in Cairo. Her broken bones began to mend and she was comfortable, and after the first week Kerim paid frequent visits to the hospital to sit and talk with her. He knew that she was unlikely to receive any other visitors, apart from official questioning, and together with his vague feeling of responsibility for her was the common bond of a dangerous trade and a joint exile from their Egyptian homeland. There were many similarities in their backgrounds which drew them close, and as the life and colour slowly returned to Schererzade's face, Kerim could not fail to notice that she became increasingly more lovely. She had been one of the most sought-after dancers in Cairo, and he could see now that her former beauty would return.

They kept no secrets from each other, and during their afternoon talks Kerim was able to piece together the disjointed details of her career. Schererzade had taken her first unwitting step into the sordid world of spying in 1952, during the period immediately before the evacuation of the Suez Canal Zone by the British Army. She had then been dancing in a very minor night club in Port Said, and there had been no thought of spying in her mind. Instead she had fallen in love with a young British officer, and it was her honest concern for his safety that had led her to warn him of the violent threats and plots that were uttered against the British. The young officer had eventually been recalled to England and their love affair had ended, but not before he had introduced her to Jackson, then a Captain but already an Intelligence man. The rumours, hostile talk and tit bits of information which she constantly heard at the club she then passed on not for love but for money.

Jackson had made good use of her again during the Suez landings of 1956. By then her dancing career had progressed and she was working in Cairo, where again she was in a position to overhear a great many items of value. At this time she was not in direct contact with Jackson, and was passing on her reports through an intermediary agent. The middleman had proved to be a double agent who was also working for Israel, and as Schererzade's carefully gathered scraps of small talk became of less interest to the British after their retreat from Suez, they increased in their value to the Israelies. Soon Schererzade was working directly and only for Israel.

She was still a dancer, and now she danced at the fashionable *Ali Baba*, a club that was greatly favoured by the young officers of Nasser's army during their free time in Cairo. Here she also became the mistress of Colonel Hamid Mehran, one of the army's top-ranking staff officers, and through him she achieved what was to be her greatest coup and her final downfall. Mehran had been closely connected with the detailed planning for a future military attack and invasion of Israel, and Schererzade had taken the opportunity to photograph the documents concerned after a night of love-making at the Colonel's apartment.

Unfortunately her career was almost at an end, for she had already aroused the suspicions of the Egyptian security police. At that stage there was no definite evidence against her, and her position as Mehran's mistress had made her safe from any premature arrest and interrogation, but it did not save her from the murder attempt when she had been deliberately knocked down by the black car. The incident had happened late at night in the back alley, the car driving at her without lights and continuing without a stop after she had been smashed to one side.

A young Englishman and his wife had come to her aid, and in her pain and desperation she had given them the film of the Mehran documents.[1] After that she had passed out, but she had lived to recover consciousness in the Cairo hospital. Her knowledge of the subsequent events was very hazy, and limited to what she had been told by the cruel-faced Major of security police who had come to interrogate her as she

---

[1] See *Nightmare on the Nile*.

lay helplessly in her bed. Something had gone wrong and the police knew about the film; the young Englishman and his wife were in flight and were being hunted throughout Egypt, and her own position had been portrayed to her as hopeless.

That had been her position when Kerim had appeared on the scene. She realized now that the English couple must have been successful in escaping from Egypt, and that somehow they had made contact with Jackson, but she could only guess at the details. And like Kerim she could only wonder at Jackson's purpose in deciding to save her.

Kerim's own story was only a little less vivid. His early life had been spent in Cairo where his father had settled down to run a small café after marrying his Egyptian mother. He had been initially recruited by the C.I.A., and had worked for the Americans for six years before his activities had been uncovered by the Egyptian security police. Then he had been forced to flee from Egypt. His father had been brutally shot dead while helping him to escape, and a personal vendetta had taken him into Morocco, where he had killed his man and again been obliged to make a hasty exit.[1] This time he carried a souvenir bullet neatly wedged below his left collar bone, and had needed a period of convalescence in the United States before he had been sent back to the Middle East. He had made his base in Beirut where problems of joint Anglo-American interest had brought him into contact with Jackson. For his own security he found that he preferred the tighter network of British Intelligence to the more sprawling organization of the C.I.A., and when Jackson had approached him with the offer of a permanent job he had agreed.

All this he told Schererzade as she lay back against her pillows, and afterwards he wondered why he had been so frank. It was unwise, unnecessary, and possibly even dangerous to reveal too many facts about himself to anyone, and yet still he

------

[1] See *Murder in Marrakech*.

did not feel that he had been indiscreet. At that time he was not fully aware that he was falling in love.

* * *

For six weeks Schererzade lay flat upon her back, but the operations she had endured in Cairo had been successful with no complications, and at last her British doctors began the task of teaching her to walk again. The process continued as slowly and painfully as before, but with a carefully planned programme of exercises and physical therapy they gradually taught her to stand with the aid of crutches. Kerim saw her daily, offering endless encouragement, and finally persuaded her doctors to allow him to take her on excursions outside the hospital. He hired a car to take her to the local beauty spots outside Nicosia, where they could breathe deeply on the fresh, pine-scented air, and absorb the full warmth of the hot Mediterranean sun. Cyprus was an excellent spot in which to convalesce, and through these outings Schererzade began to move more rapidly towards full health.

They lay one afternoon on the grassy slope of a hill, shaded from the full heat of the sun by a giant cedar tree. Below them was a small whitewashed village, almost hidden amongst golden oak, alder and olive groves. It was siesta time and nothing stirred. The heat was drowsy and only one bird found the energy to sing, warbling almost breathlessly in a nearby clump of greenery.

Schererzade lay still upon the tartan rug that Kerim had spread out upon the grass. Her eyes were closed and she appeared to be asleep. She was dressed in a simple blue skirt and cardigan that had been borrowed from one of her nurses, for as yet she had no clothes of her own, and he thought that the colour suited her. Her long, dark hair was spread in a careless pool around her neck and shoulders, and he felt a strange temptation to caress the silk-like strands between his fingers. She sensed that he was watching her, and quietly her eyelids flickered open.

Kerim smiled, feeling rather like a schoolboy who has been startled from the contemplation of some minor crime. He shifted slightly as he leaned on the elbow, and searched for some pretence at natural conversation.

'Schererzade,' he said. 'That's quite an exotic name, your mother must have read the Arabian Nights.'

She smiled. 'It is not the name my mother gave me. It is a name I adopted when I became a dancer. It is necessary for a dancer to have an exotic name. Besides, my mother could not read. She was a very primitive woman.'

Kerim was silent for a moment, and then he asked:

'Is your mother still alive? Do you have any family in Egypt?'

She made a negative movement of her head. 'No. There is no one. My father died when I was small, my mother when I was fourteen. That was when I had to become a dancer.' She paused for a moment, and then said seriously, 'My mother was a witch.'

Kerim looked faintly startled, and was

not sure whether he should smile. He said doubtfully:

'What sort of a witch?'

Schererzade was no longer returning his gaze, instead she was looking up into the twisted branches of the cedar tree above their heads. She said quietly:

'My mother was an old Nubian woman. She had a strange power. She knew things. I did not inherit her features, those came from my father who was Arab, but I do have some of her power. I know things before they happen.'

'You mean that you can tell the future?'

'No.' Again she faintly shook her head. 'But I know things. I can tell when it is safe to trust someone, and when someone means me harm. And when things happen, I know what they mean. In Cairo, when I performed my last dance at the *Ali Baba*, I knew that it was the last time that I would ever dance there. I did not know what was going to happen, but I knew that I would never dance there again. And in the hospital, when you first stood over me and told

31

me that you would get me to safety, I knew that it would be so. I did not know who you were, or how or why you would help me, but I knew that what you said was the truth.'

She became silent and closed her eyes as though unwilling to go on. Kerim waited, sensing that this was not the right moment to interrupt, and then she said:

'There is something that I know now.'

Kerim hesitated, and then asked:

'What do you know?'

'I know when something is ending. I know that this is our last afternoon together, here, on this island.' Her voice was very low, and after a moment she turned her head to look at him. 'I know that you are going away.'

Kerim looked into her dark, serious eyes, and somewhat uncertainly he laughed.

'There is no reason why I should leave Cyprus. And if there were, how could you possibly know in advance?'

'I know,' she replied simply. 'And it will be so.'

There was a sadness in her voice and in her eyes. She lay motionless, and slowly, strangely, Kerim believed her. Their faces were close, their bodies almost touching, and suddenly he realized that while he had been listening to her his hand had strayed to tangle absently in her dark hair. It was not the right moment, and yet it was the right moment, and very gently he kissed her.

When he drew back he still did not know what to say. They lingered for a little longer on the shaded hillside, but when the afternoon grew cooler he lifted her in his arms and carried her back to their car which stood nearby. He propped cushions behind her to support her back during the drive to Nicosia, and then he returned to pick up the tartan car rug. He stood for a moment, feeling disturbed and thoughtful as he stared down the slope at the white houses nestling amongst the green groves, and then he turned away.

That same night Jackson re-entered their lives.

3

Back To Work

It was late in the afternoon when Kerim returned Schererzade to the hospital. A male nurse helped him to lift her from his car into a wheelchair and then take her back to her bed in the small private ward, and he waited while she was made comfortable. It was then that they were told that she had another visitor.

For a moment they exchanged glances, and then Schererzade looked away. Kerim remembered their conversation on the hillside and again a faint disturbance seemed to vibrate through his nervous system. He told the nurse that he would wait with Schererzade, and when her visitor appeared a few moments later the nebulous feeling inside him had generated into a cool hostility. There was no surprise as he recognized Jackson.

The Major was not in uniform, instead

34

he wore a dark blue suit with a matching, hand-knitted tie. He wore no hat and his thick, sand coloured hair was showing just the merest hint of grey at the temples. His tough, middle-aged face had a friendly smile of greeting, but its effect was spoiled by seeming just a little bit unnatural. He offered a large, vigorous hand and his grip was brief but hard.

'Hello, Soiron. I didn't expect to find you still here. Expected you'd be back in Beirut by now. Still, Cyprus isn't a bad place to spend a holiday. Can't say I blame you for taking your time.'

Kerim smiled, trying to hide the coldness he felt. He knew that he had idled and wasted his time far longer than he had any right to expect, and now that the interlude had ended he had no cause to complain. He said briefly:

'There was nothing waiting for me in Beirut. There was no need to hurry.'

Jackson nodded in agreement. The nurse had left them alone and he moved past Kerim to stand by the bed, looking down at Schererzade. He studied her for a moment and then said:

'You've certainly changed since we last met. You were not much more than a girl then, and now you're a fine-looking young woman.' He paused reflectively. 'When was it? Fifty-three or fifty-four? Fifty-four, I think. After that I found it safer to stay out of Egypt and we had to do all our business through a chap called Kadish. Then Kadish mysteriously disappeared and we lost contact. I never did find out who gave Kadish the chop.' He smiled again, and then finished quietly. 'They tell me you've had a tough time. I'm glad you're getting better.'

Schererzade returned the smile a little nervously.

'I have to thank you,' she said, 'for sending Kerim into Egypt to save my life.'

'It was the least I could do. You were very valuable to me in fifty-two, and again in fifty-six, and despite our image some of us do have memories and a sense of gratitude to our friends.' He drew up a chair to sit down beside her and added,

'Besides, I didn't actually stick my neck out. I merely asked Kerim if he cared to have a crack at it.'

There was an awkward pause of silence which Jackson did not appear to notice. Kerim moved closer to the foot of the bed but said nothing, waiting. Schererzade touched her tongue to her lips, wetting them, and then asked:

'Major Jackson, why are you here?'

Jackson smiled, but did not answer directly.

'I would have come earlier,' he said. 'But I've been rather busy just lately. My present base is in Aden which is where your two young friends eventually appeared with your roll of film. It was rather fortunate really that I was on the spot. If anyone else had handled it they might not have realized that you were the same Schererzade who had served us so well in the past, in which case you might still be in Cairo. However, all's well that ends well.'

'But why are you here?' Schererzade persisted. 'You have come for Kerim, haven't you?'

Jackson regarded her with shrewd blue eyes, and then looked back to Kerim.

'Frankly, no,' he said. 'I wasn't aware that Kerim was still in Nicosia. As I said before I had rather expected him to be back in Beirut. I'm afraid Aden's been a bit hectic lately, the terrorism is getting out of hand and I haven't been able to keep as well informed as usual on the other spheres of the Middle East.'

He looked down at Schererzade again and went on:

'But you are right in thinking that I did not come all the way to Cyprus without a purpose. I came to see you.'

'But why? I have talked to your Intelligence officers here. I have told them everything that I know. You have the film of Hamid Mehran's documents. What more can you want?'

Jackson tugged at his jaw for a moment, and then said quietly:

'I've been talking to your doctors. They tell me that you are now making a very fast recovery. Soon you will be able to walk without the aid of crutches, and then they will be able to discharge you

38

from the hospital. I am hoping that then you will be able to work for me again.'

'You mean — to do some more spying!'

Jackson nodded. 'Frankly, yes.'

'But that is impossible!' Schererzade twisted her shoulders on the bed so that she could face him more fully. Her face reflected more surprise and bewilderment than alarm and she continued, 'Perhaps I will walk, but surely they must have told you that I will never dance again. I cannot get another job such as I had before, and even if I could dance it would be crazy for me to return to Cairo!'

Jackson smiled. 'I would not ask you to. It was not Egypt that I had in mind.'

Kerim had listened and the cold hostility inside him had grown. Now he interrupted bluntly:

'Any other Arab country would be equally as dangerous. She has been marked down by the Egyptians. Surely you do not think that they will not warn their allies. To send her into Syria or Jordan would be equally as fatal. She would be dead within a week.'

Jackson gave him an appraising glance. He had measured Kerim's feeling now but if he felt any annoyance it did not show. He said calmly:

'I appreciate your point, and I certainly wouldn't send her into any of the Arab countries.'

'Then she is of no use to you. As with me it is only her knowledge of Arabic, and the fact that she is Arab and can mingle freely in those countries that makes her of value. Outside the Middle East her value would be lost.'

Jackson smiled. 'Kerim, there is a part of the Middle East which you seem to have overlooked. A part where she will be relatively safe.' He turned his attention back to Schererzade and finished. 'What I am asking is whether you are prepared to carry out any farther espionage work for me? This time in Israel.'

'Israel!' Schererzade was startled.

Jackson nodded. 'That's right. We know that you've been working for the Israelies for the past few years. That film of the Mehran documents was originally intended for Israel, it only reached me because things went wrong and you had to get rid of it fast. However, that wasn't your fault, and as I have notified your Israeli friends of the contents of those documents they have no reason to be displeased with you. In your present circumstances you have nowhere to go when you are eventually discharged from this hospital, and it would not be an unnatural thing if you applied to Israel for asylum. Once you are legally in the country I think I can arrange a job for you in Tel Aviv. Again it will be in a night club, but this time you will not have to dance. This club engages a certain number of hostesses, whose only duty is to sit with the customers and coax them into buying more drinks. You're a very attractive young woman and should manage that quite easily, and you should be in an even better position for collecting careless talk and information than you were in the *Ali Baba* in Cairo.'

Schererzade stared at him, and then looked helplessly towards Kerim. The young French-Egyptian looked deep into

41

her eyes. He was silent and his mouth was tight, but she knew that he was willing her to refuse. It was then that she knew how she must answer, and she lowered her gaze to look down at the blue-patterned bedspread that covered her lower limbs. She hesitated for a moment, but when she raised her head again she avoided Kerim's opposing grey eyes and spoke to Jackson.

She said quietly. 'Why do you wish me to spy against Israel? I have always believed that Britain and Israel were friends.'

'They are,' Jackson replied. 'But even with our friends we like to keep our intelligence reports up to date. The Middle East is a very sensitive spot and there are signs that the old tensions are building up again. War is like a dark, angry cloud on the horizon. You can see it coming before it actually breaks. That cloud is forming now, and that's why I must try to be fully informed of what is happening on both sides. I need to know what Israel means to do, just as much as I need to know what the Arabs mean

42

to do. That's my job, and by doing it I might enable the British Government to exert some influence over coming events. I don't have much hope of that, but it's still my job to keep them fully supplied with hard facts, however the situation might develop.'

Kerim said slowly, 'You mean that you anticipate another Arab-Israeli war?'

Jackson turned on his chair, watched him for a moment, and then nodded.

'That's exactly what I'm anticipating. It's been boiling up for a long time. Russia has deliberately been pouring arms into all the Arab states and now they are itching to go out and use them. There's talk of a *jihad*, a holy war, to annihilate the whole state of Israel and sweep the Jews into the sea. As you probably know, those documents Schererzade managed to photograph revealed the details of a full-scale military campaign devised against Israel by Egypt. I'm absolutely certain that before long the whole mess is going to explode.'

He paused for a moment, and then continued ruefully. 'When I first saw the contents of those photographs I thought that we held a very good controlling hand. I made sure that the Egyptians knew that we had the photographs and could use them to prove any attack she made against Israel as preplanned aggression. I also made sure that the Israelies knew the basic details so that they could strengthen the weak points in their defences and would know what to expect. However, I was too damned optimistic. The Egyptians have probably decided that they can denounce the photographs as forgeries in the event of any international inquest after the war, and so they are going ahead. Now I honestly don't think that anything can stop a third Arab-Israeli conflict from taking place.'

Kerim said bluntly, 'If nothing can stop it, then why is it necessary for Schererzade to go into Israel?'

'Because although nothing can stop it, it will soon be over. The actual war will be quick and savage, but neither side can afford to wage it for long. Afterwards the pieces will have to be picked up and another attempt made to stabilize the Middle East. We still have to bring some sort of peace to this area. Be cynical if you like and say that this is only because of western oil interests, or the need for free passage through the Suez Canal, but that is our aim. We can only do it, or try to do it, by being in full possession of all the facts, and that's why we still need intelligence reports from inside Israel, as well as from the surrounding Arab states.'

Jackson stopped again and looked at each of his listeners in turn, his manner enquiring whether there were any more questions. There were none, and finally he looked down again at Schererzade.

'That was a rather condensed account of the present situation, but it should give you some idea of why I'm asking you to go into Israel. The job will be no more dangerous than before, just a matter of keeping your eyes and ears open and reporting anything that you think might be useful. You've been very good at it in the past, and I think that it was just bad luck that you were caught out in Cairo.'

He smiled at her. 'Will you work for me in Tel Aviv?'

Kerim watched for her answer, feeling a strange tension in his middle as he moved along the bedside to stand close beside Jackson's shoulder. Schererzade lay motionless and despite his concentrated stare she avoided his eyes. She refused to look at either of them, and then she said in a low voice:

'Yes, Major. I will go to Tel Aviv.'

Kerim's mouth tightened for he had hoped that she would give a negative answer. Her assent had disappointed him and he did not understand why. There was no need for her to endanger her life by undertaking any farther spying, and apart from his concern for her safety there was an even deeper feeling that somehow she had let him down. He didn't understand it and so he said nothing.

Jackson was still smiling, looking like a tough but considerate father. He reached out and patted Schererzade's arm where it lay limply outside her bedclothes and said:

'Fine. I knew that I could rely on you. And now that your future is nicely settled let's hope that you'll hurry up and make a full recovery. With luck you'll be walking and taking up your new job in Tel Aviv in a matter of weeks.'

Schererzade made a slight, affirmative movement of her head, but did not speak. Jackson hesitated a little awkwardly, and then straightened up from her bedside. He turned to face Kerim and then said casually:

'As a matter of fact, Kerim, I'm glad that you're here and not in Beirut. It's saved me the necessity of making a detour on my way back and having to explain the whole Middle East situation all over again. You have to know it because I've also got a little job of work for you.'

It was Kerim's turn to hesitate. He almost asked for details of the job, but suddenly he knew that the details did not matter. The holiday was over and it was time for him to go back to work. There was nothing for him here on Cyprus. He breathed in deeply and said:

'I too am ready, wherever you want to send me.'

'Glad to hear it,' Jackson responded cheerfully. 'But I think I'd better explain to you elsewhere. Schererzade must be tired and we've already disturbed enough of her rest.'

Kerim nodded, and he failed to notice the unhappiness in Schererzade's dark, saddened eyes before she closed them and turned her face slightly away towards her pillow. She had chosen to accept Jackson's offer because she knew full well that Kerim had begun to fall in love with her. And she knew she was not fit for him. When she had first danced she had performed naked in a sordid sideshow, and since then her body had known many men. She had betrayed her last lover after being his mistress for many months, and now she felt tainted and unclean. For Kerim's sake it was best that their friendship should be ended, and Jackson had given her the opportunity to end it. However, it still pained her to find that Kerim was willing to let it end without a fight.

4

Damascus

Kerim left Cyprus the following day, departing from Nicosia airport as a tourist class passenger on a noon flight to Damascus. Schererzade remained behind and there had been no opportunity for him to see her again. Jackson had waited for him when he had said goodbye to her in the hospital the previous evening and so their parting had been brief and unsatisfactory. He was still a gloomy and disillusioned young man, but she had made her choice and he saw no other course for himself but to return to his own job. He was glad now that Jackson had provided a job for him.

They had returned to his apartment after leaving the hospital, and there Jackson had gone into even deeper detail on the current situation between Israel and the surrounding Arab states.

It was an almost endless list of border incidents, night infiltration, sabotage and murder attacks by the Syrians, Egyptians and Jordanians, and savage reprisals by the Israelies. The United Nations peace keeping forces posted along the troublesome frontiers were having less and less effect, and it was Jackson's considered opinion that they were fighting a losing battle. The Army man had talked for over an hour while Kerim listened patiently, explaining the whole Arab-Jewish problem which both of them well knew, and then finally he came to the job he had in mind.

They sat facing each other in two large and slightly sagging armchairs, sipping coffee as they talked. Kerim had already refilled the cups three times from the percolator in the tiny kitchen, and Jackson had eaten most of the opened packet of cream biscuits that lay on the small table between them. The Major paused to take another biscuit, drank more of his coffee and then placed his cup on the table.

'That's the general situation,' he said. 'Now we come to my part in it, and yours. In my case I've been told to forget about Aden. It's no longer the number one problem, and I have to concentrate on sifting the intelligence reports on the increasing tension between Israel and her neighbours. I've been doing that for the past few weeks, and among other things I've got men watching all the main airports in the Middle East. They keep a lookout for any known agents and troublemakers, and it's also useful to know which of the sheikhs and politicians are visiting which capital. It's the first step to finding out why. Recently there's been a lot more traffic between Cairo, Damascus and Amman, and we've had reason to become interested in a certain Egyptian gentleman who has made several return flights between Cairo and Damascus. According to the passenger lists his name is Mahmoud Abdel Rashid and he's a civil engineer. His passport probably says the same but I wouldn't believe that either. Anyway, Rashid, or whatever his name is, was watched. We don't know who he contacted because our interest wasn't

51

fully aroused until he had made his third trip. He arrived for the fourth time about ten days ago, and this time he didn't have a return ticket. He had a companion with him, travelling under the name of Ahmed Barek. They were met by a car outside the airport and driven away pretty smartly. My boy managed to get the number, and after a couple of days we traced the car to a large villa outside Damascus. It's that villa that interests me now.'

Jackson stopped, helped himself to another biscuit, and then continued as precisely as before.

'I did some checking up on that villa, and found that it had recently been up for sale and had been purchased for a large sum of money. More than it was worth, which seemed to indicate that someone wanted it rather urgently. The name of the buyer was obviously a front, and nobody seems to know anything about the new owners. There was one little coincidence, however. The date of the sale coincided with Rashid's third visit to Damascus.'

'So now you think that Rashid and

Barek are residing in the villa?'

'That's right. I'm not sure but it's a pretty safe bet. The villa has some extensive private grounds. It's encircled by a high wall, and it's well guarded. None of my men have been able to penetrate inside, but their reports indicate that the villa also accommodates over a dozen mysterious Syrians who have gathered there for some unknown purpose. I want to know what that purpose is? I want to know why Rashid and Barek were sent from Cairo? I want to know exactly what is happening behind those walls? And I want you to find out.'

Kerim said slowly, 'Why me? Why not one of your local agents on the spot?'

'For two reasons. One is because I haven't a man to spare for a continuous watch on the villa. And two is that I don't want to take the unnecessary risk of compromising a local agent. If anything goes wrong with you I can pull you out and return you to Beirut, or use you in some other capital, whereas most of my contacts in Damascus have homes and families there. They are permanent and can't be so easily moved about. Besides,' he smiled briefly. 'I think that you are more capable of doing a better job. You're a professional.'

Kerim gazed steadily into the shrewd blue eyes that awaited his answer, and he was not impressed by the note of flattery that had marked the end of Jackson's little speech. He said at last:

'All right, I will go to Damascus for you.'

Jackson watched him for a moment, sensing his cold lack of enthusiasm. Then he decided to let it pass and smiled.

'That's settled then. You'll fly to Damascus tomorrow and I'll arrange for a place where you can stay. One of my friends there has a spare room where you won't be too noticeable.' He glanced at the empty biscuit packet and finished. 'Now I think it would be a good idea to go out and eat. I'll buy you a drink at the same time.'

★ ★ ★

The flight was smooth, and although Jackson accompanied him they made very little conversation. Kerim had gazed moodily through his window, watching the blue of the Mediterranean passing below flimsy white patterns of thin cloud; then the lush green valleys and pine sloped mountains of the Lebanon, giving way gradually to the brown and rust-red hills of Syria. Soon after Cyprus had fallen away behind them a stewardess had offered them a choice of orange juice or coffee. They had both accepted coffee, and since then had remained silent until the plane approached Damascus. When the order came for them to fasten their safety belts Jackson said casually:

'I radioed Damascus last night so you are expected. The place you want is number thirty-seven, Darrasa Street. That's near The Street Called Straight in the old part of the city. The man who lives there is reliable. His name is George and he'll fix you up with anything you need.'

Kerim stared at him.

'You mean that you are not coming?'

Jackson grinned. 'Sorry, I can't spare the time. I'm staying with the plane through to Amman. Aden's a bit too far away so I've had to set up a new base there.' He saw the doubt written in Kerim's face and added, 'Don't worry about George. His house is safe. He'll be at home waiting for you so there will be no difficulty in making contact. You don't need me to personally introduce you.'

The plane was landing and there was no opportunity for Kerim to argue. He tightened his belt with an angry jerk and then they touched down. The twin jets roared as the big airliner thundered along the flashing runway and then slowly she braked to a stop. As they unfastened their safety belts a pleasant voice over the intercom thanked all departing passengers for their company, and requested continuing passengers to leave the plane and wait in the transit lounge until it left for Amman in thirty minutes time. The message came over three times, in English, French and Arabic, and while the passengers were shuffling out Jackson turned to Kerim and briefly offered his hand.

'I'll wish you luck here,' he said. 'There'll be eyes watching once we step down on to the runway.'

Kerim nodded, and after a brief handshake Jackson stood up, straightened his tie and then mingled with the other passengers filing down the centre of the long cabin. Kerim gave him a few minutes to get clear and then followed.

Outside the sun was brilliant, and he had to blink his eyes rapidly on leaving the shadowed interior of the aircraft. Ahead of him his fellow passengers had split into two groups and it was easy to pick out Jackson's thick, sandy hair from the smaller party entering the transit lounge. The Major was walking briskly and did not look back.

For the next fifteen minutes there was the inevitable delay of customs and passport control. Kerim carried a Lebanese passport that defined him as a journalist and a native of Beirut. It was scrutinised dubiously, but stamped without comment, while behind him an innocent Arab with Semitic features was hostilely questioned on whether he had ever visited Israel.

Kerim moved on to collect his one small suitcase that had now been disgorged from the plane, and waited patiently while a customs man pawed through its contents. He carried two cameras, a 35 millimetre Halina and a second-hand Leica for more detailed press work, for photo-journalism was both his hobby and his cover, and these involved him in a delay over duplicate declaration forms. Then at last he was able to escape from the airport and hail a taxi.

He named a hotel on the wide Baghdad Boulevard in the modern part of the city and relaxed to enjoy the drive. When the taxi stopped he paid it off, walked a hundred yards along the street and hailed another. This time he named The Street Called Straight and was taken into the older part of Damascus. It was a journey back into time, for the city was one of the oldest inhabited sites on earth, and had been capital of Syria in biblical times. The Street Called Straight ran east-west for almost a mile, cutting a direct line through the souks and bazaars, and guarded by ancient Roman gateways at either end. Kerim stopped his taxi at the eastern gateway, and proceeded to search for Darrasa Street on foot.

It took him thirty minutes to find the place he wanted. Darrasa Street proved to be one of the branching lanes through the maze of old houses to the south of the bazaars. It was narrow and dusty, smelling of the dung left by passing donkeys, and number thirty-seven was reached through an arched alleyway where Kerim had to hold his suitcase in front of him in order to move forward. An old Arab woman, invisible in a grey shroud except for her prying eyes, pointed out a flight of wooden steps in answer to his query. She watched him climb and then squeezed past and hurried on.

There was a wooden door at the head of the steps, with the number thirty-seven written in chalk in Arabic numerals. It opened before Kerim could knock and a man appeared. He was young and wore dark trousers and a spotless white shirt opened at the neck. He favoured a small moustache, and there was a thin gold chain around his throat. He smiled nervously and aroused an instant dislike. The smile was too sensual.

'I think you must be Soiron. Please come in.'

He spoke in English, fluently and a little proud. Kerim accepted the invitation and walked past him as he drew back into the dark interior of the building. It was cool inside, and when the door was closed they faced each other for a strained moment. Kerim thought that Jackson had no taste in friends.

'I am George.' The young Syrian broke the silence. He offered a slim hand and Kerim noticed the gold bangle that adorned the almost white wrist.

'I am Kerim Soiron,' he said. He shook hands reluctantly.

George smiled as though they had become instant friends.

'I am glad to see you. Major Jackson informed me that you would be arriving so all is ready for you. I live here alone with my mother. She speaks only Arabic so you need not be afraid that she will overhear us while we talk in English. She lives on the lower floor of this house, while I have the two rooms upstairs. One of those rooms is now yours.'

Kerim glanced round the room. Noticing the single bed in the corner, the simple washstand and the pin-up photographs of male film stars that decorated the walls. George watched him, hoping for a sign of approval and showing his disappointment when he saw none.

Kerim said, 'It's a nice place,' but there was no feeling in his words. He looked curiously at his host and asked, 'What's your line of business, apart from your connection with Jackson?'

George smiled. 'I am a guide. I show the foreign tourists around Damascus. Also I have an uncle who owns a shop in the bazaar. I take the tourists there and I get commision on anything they buy. It is a good business. Sometimes there are girls, European and American girls, who are lonely. They want to make love. It is easy. And sometimes there are men.'

Kerim nodded and turned away. He picked up his case and said:

'You'd better show me my room. I'll get settled in.'

He knew all that he wanted to know about George.

★ ★ ★

For the next few days he was very busy with his cameras. He knew that it was unwise to rush into the actual job in hand before he had got the feel of his background and could sense whether he was being observed, and he needed to build up evidence of his legal journalistic activities in order to back up his cover should anything go wrong. He worked as a freelance but was known to several glossy magazines, including a few on the American market. Once he had even sold a set of photographs to *Life*, but he was not as successful as he would have liked to have been. The sales of his pictures made a bonus, but they could not match the direct pay that came from Jackson.

He spent the first day in working out

themes for his articles, and then began taking his pictures. The teeming life of the bazaars, gave him an endless variety of subjects, both in its people and its merchandise. The tiny shops were filled with the scent of spices, with old silver and hand-crafted copper and brass, with dates and figs and crystallized fruits, and with the famous Damascus silks and brocades. The streets were a dark warren roofed with high arches, and in contrast were the hot sunlit courtyards of the mosques. Kerim worked for three days in the city and then hired a car in order to visit its outer limits. After two more days he had enough material for his needs and he was also satisfied that no one was taking any particular notice of his movements. He deemed it time to turn his attention to his main purpose.

George accompanied him as he drove out of Damascus to take his first look at the villa. So far he had resisted all the attempts of the young Syrian to 'guide' him, but on this occasion he had no choice. He had to be sure that he found the right place and he could not afford to make his presence known by asking directions in the area. George was pleased and sat closer to him than was necessary, talking inanely throughout the journey.

As they left the city the road forced a dusty path through olive groves and fruit orchards. The sun was hot and directly overhead, and Kerim wore dark glasses to protect his eyes from the glare. He was sweating, but beside him George appeared to be cool. They passed several small buildings, and then George pointed out a long, ten-foot wall that showed through a screen of silver-green olive groves. Kerim slowed the car and drove more slowly past the entrance to a private roadway of hard-packed earth, but there was a turn in the track and he could not see the gateway through the walls. The villa itself was hidden behind its protective barrier.

Kerim drove on another half mile and then stopped the car, an old grey Mercedes that was dusty enough to merge into the general landscape without being too noticeable. He got out and straightened his back, and George came

64

to stand beside him.

'What are you planning, Kerim?'

Kerim said nothing. George had dropped easily into the habit of calling him by his first name, but without damaging their working relationship he could not afford to be unfriendly. He stared up at the low hills that now climbed away from the road on their left. The villa was on the same side farther back but the level orchards and olive groves had ended at the foot of the more rugged slopes. He noted the scanty cover of grey rocks, a few low bushes and clumps of alder and wild oak which was all that broke the bareness of the brown earth, and he was thoughtful for a moment before he looked back at his companion.

'I'm going to take a walk up there. I'll borrow your binoculars and perhaps I can find a vantage point that overlooks the villa.'

George nodded approval and went back to the car. His movements were quick and eager and he returned with the leather binocular case slung by its strap around his neck. Kerim saw that he intended to come along but decided not to argue.

They had to walk through the last of the thinning olive groves before they reached the foot of the hillside, and here they found a narrow footpath leading upwards. It was simply a twisting ribbon of white dust, but although Kerim noted footprints and donkey droppings they passed no one. The sun blazed from a vivid blue sky and Kerim was panting by the time the path began to level out, and even George was beginning to lose his relaxed air.

They stopped where a bundle of oak saplings gave them some shade, and surveyed their surroundings. Below them was a level expanse of dusty green, the fertile orchards and groves. To the right was the straight boundary of the road, and to the left the continuing circle of the hills. Half a mile distant the villa and its enclosed grounds were visible, with the olive groves pressing close against its four walls. The villa was a large two-storied building with iron-railed balconies, a long verandah and a flat roof.

Kerim turned to take the binoculars. He did not have to ask for them for George had already taken them out of the leather case and was handing them towards him. They were ex British Army field glasses, and almost certainly supplied by Jackson, although why George should need them in the ordinary course of his activities was beyond Kerim's comprehension. His first thought was that they were probably used privately for spying through bedroom windows.

Through the glasses he could examine the villa and the grounds much more closely. At first it appeared to be deserted, but when he focused on the large, iron-grilled gateway that gave entrance to the grounds he saw that there was a movement in the small gatehouse beside it. Through the open door he could just distinguish the one man on guard. There would be no need to guard an empty house, and so he made a closer scrutiny of the villa. Only two of its windows were unshuttered, but even so he could see nothing inside. Then another movement drew his attention to the doorway.

Two men appeared, tough, young and capable looking. They wore nothing but shorts and sunglasses as they stepped down from the verandah and strolled across the lawn. Kerim watched their progress and then saw that there were other, almost identical figures sunbathing on the grass. They were half hidden by a patch of shrubbery and he had not noticed them before. There were five men in all, and although he could not get all their faces into full focus he was sure that none of them matched the descriptions he had been given of Rashid and Barek. He watched for another ten minutes, but no one else appeared. The five men did nothing more sinister than to rub oil upon each others shoulders, and at last Kerim returned the binoculars to George.

The young Syrian raised them to study the villa for himself, pouted his lips thoughtfully and then lowered the glasses again.

'What do you think?' he asked.

'I think we should go back before someone notices the car,' Kerim said calmly. 'Tomorrow morning we'll drive out here again and you can take the car back to Damascus. I'll spend the day up here and you can come out and collect me again in the evening.'

George looked disappointed that nothing more dramatic was to happen, but he made no argument. He returned the binoculars to their case and Kerim led the way down the hillside.

★ ★ ★

The following day Kerim spent fourteen tedious hours of patiently watching the villa. He chose one of the thicker clumps of trees for his hiding place, a spot where he could lay flat on his stomach in the shade and look straight down the hillside. The path was below him and although it was occasionally used by passing Arabs, mostly in the early morning and late afternoon, he could see them coming long before they were in a position to see him. He had come well fortified with a water bottle, a flask of coffee and a packet of food, but even so he was tired, hungry and thirsty when the day was over.

He had also learned nothing. The villa had been silent and apparently empty throughout the whole of the morning, and there was only a solitary guard dozing in the gatehouse to indicate that it was still inhabited. At noon a relief had appeared for the guard, and then there had been another period of stillness. Finally there had been a stirring of life and a group of men had appeared to relax and sunbathe on the lawns, following the pattern of the previous day. They were all young, a cheerful, comradely company who appeared to have nothing definite to do. As the afternoon grew cooler they began to play games and physical exercises, and it was obvious that they were all very fit and active. Then at six o'clock they all disappeared into the villa again and he observed nothing more. An hour later Kerim descended the hillside to meet George with the Mercedes, a puzzled and irritable man.

Over the next few days the pattern was unchanged, and Kerim remained mystified. He had counted up to thirteen hardy young Syrian Arabs, all fitting approximately into the twenty to thirty-five age group, and he had also caught a brief glimpse of a darker man with a pock-marked face whom he was sure must be Ahmed Barek. The Egyptian had appeared once in the grounds to talk earnestly to one of the Syrians, but had returned almost immediately to the villa. Of Mahmoud Abdel Rashid there was no sign, but Kerim had the feeling that he was somewhere in the house.

He was tempted to move closer and penetrate into the villa grounds, but one deterrent held him back. His observations had not failed to notice the small, fenced-in enclosure in one corner of the grounds where four large wolfhounds were kept chained. If they scented an intruder they would bark, and if they were released that intruder would be finished.

After a week Kerim changed his tactics. He slept during the day, for he was sure that the occupants of the villa must be doing likewise, and he watched from the hillside at night. He began his vigil at dusk, and waited another three hours before anything happened. The villa was in darkness, but sounds of muffled movement told him that some kind of activity had commenced.

The starlight enabled him to see, but not very well, and his eyes ached as he held his glasses on the villa. Then a car engine started up and abruptly the grounds were bathed with the bright splash of headlights. Kerim saw that there were two cars, and then a third appeared from the garage behind the villa. All three were rapidly filled with men and then the small convoy began to move off. The gates were opened and the three beams of light moved through the olive groves to the main road, turning left and then roaring away into the night.

Kerim sat up, still mystified, but feeling that he was making just a little progress.

5

The Training Ground

Kerim maintained his watch throughout the night, but there was little reward for his efforts. The villa was empty and in pitch darkness, and only the guard on the gate was left. He noticed that the guard had been doubled and that the dogs had been let loose in the grounds, so there was no hope of entering the villa while the bulk of its inhabitants was absent. Fortunately it was a warm night so he was not uncomfortable, and as he knew that the sound of the cars would awaken him he allowed himself to doze through the early hours after midnight. The sound of the returning convoy disturbed him an hour before dawn and he watched as the three sets of headlights turned off the main road and swept a path through the olives to illuminate the gateway of the villa. One of the guards went forward to pull open the heavy iron gates, and through his binoculars Kerim saw that the second man was standing back with a sten gun held at the ready. It was the first time that he had noticed any weapons, and he guessed that the sten must be normally kept in the gatehouse out of sight.

There was an exchange of words, apparently cheerful and relaxed but too far away to be heard. Then the small convoy re-entered the villa grounds and rolled to a stop. The passengers clambered out in a disorderly fashion, some of them yawning, and now that the sky was beginning to lighten towards dawn Kerim could make out the metallic glint of more weapons amongst them. The men moved off in a body into the villa, and then the cars drove in single file round to the garage at the back of the building. There was the sound of doors being slammed and then the three drivers returned and followed their companions into the house. The door closed behind them and once more the villa was wrapped in stillness.

Kerim looked towards the gateway and saw that it had been closed and locked, the guards were no longer visible but were almost certainly in the gatehouse. He noticed then that the dogs were now chained up behind their enclosure, and guessed that they had been recalled while he had dozed shortly before the three cars had returned.

He lowered the binoculars on to the grass in front of him and closed his eyes. He was tempted to rub them but he knew that that would not ease the ache. He was thoughtful for a moment and then looked back at the villa. The sky was a pinkish-grey in the east and the squared silhouette showed distinctly, brooding and silent behind the high protective walls that encircled the grounds. He knew from his previous observations that there would be nothing to watch now. The men inside the villa would sleep until mid-afternoon.

He stood up and stretched his aching muscles, and then he gathered up his binoculars and his empty coffee flask. He made the routine check to ensure that he had left no traces of his presence behind and then descended from the hill, avoiding the path in case he should encounter some early-rising labourer on his way to work. He had to wait for half an hour in the olive grove by the roadside before George appeared to pick him up in the old Mercedes, and by then the dawn was well advanced.

★ ★ ★

During the following two nights Kerim watched repeat performances of the strange, nocturnal events at the villa. They told him nothing except that he had to take his investigations one stage further and attempt to follow the three cars on one of their midnight expeditions. He didn't like the idea, but he could see no other way of finishing his job. Jackson's suspicions had been proved and there was certainly something unusual taking place, but he still had to discover exactly what was happening.

He disappointed George by driving out of Damascus alone, for he had no intentions of taking the young Syrian along. If he needed help he preferred to rely upon his own skill, luck, a possible prayer and the .38 automatic he carried in the dashboard panel of the car.

It was dusk as he left the city and he stopped the old Mercedes some five hundred yards before the branching side road that led up to the villa. He was out of sight, hidden by a bend in the main road, but still within hearing. He pulled the car on to the dusty verge, got out and opened up the bonnet. To satisfy any passing traffic he unscrewed the radiator cap as though the water had overboiled, and then he waited. A few cars went past, an Arab on a bicycle, and then two juvenile herdsmen drove a flock of goats along the opposite verge. The stars came out, gathering brightness in a clear black sky, and the crickets began to murmur in the grass below the olive groves. Then at last came the sound of car engines coming down the private road from the villa.

Kerim counted the sound of the three vehicles, and faintly through the boles of the trees he saw their lights turning on to the main road. He smiled briefly and then replaced the radiator cap, closing the bonnet and getting back into his car. He listened to the sound of the small convoy moving away and then he started his own engine and drove after them.

He passed the private side road and noticed that it was empty. There was no longer any sign of life. He accelerated the old Mercedes, driving without lights and after following a bend in the road that looped around the hills that were his usual vantage point he saw the rear lights of the preceding three cars ahead of him. He dropped back then until the tiny red spots of light were only just visible, and hoped that the chase would not lead him too far. For the longer the ride lasted the more time his quarry would have to realize that they were being pursued.

Fortunately the road was reasonably well surfaced, for without lights he was not able to see any cracked or crumbling patches in the tarmac until the car crashed into them. The starlight enabled him to stay on the road but while he had to concentrate on the cars ahead he could not stay alert for flaws. He cursed softly every time the springs sagged and jolted, but his hands remained steady on the wheel.

The road ran almost straight through desolate sand hills but there were many dips and hollows where Kerim had to strain his eyes to pick out the frequently vanishing glow of the distant tail lights in the darkness. He had to drive fast to keep pace but at that hour there was no traffic. He dared not get too close or use his own headlights, but after an hour he began to fear that the men in the cars ahead must eventually notice his presence. He knew that he could not expect to remain undetected indefinitely, and he was liking less and less the dangerous game he was obliged to play.

He was almost prepared to turn back, for he had not expected the drive to last so long and the risk was becoming too great, but then he suddenly realized that the three cars had slowed and were turning off the main road. He stopped his own car and allowed the leading lights to vanish, and for several moments he sat still, thinking hard. Finally he reached into the dashboard panel and checked his automatic. The Mercedes was left-hand drive and he placed the automatic on the right-hand seat close by his hand. Then he drove on slowly.

He reached the spot where the three cars had turned off, stopped the Mercedes again, picked up the automatic and got out. There was no cover for anyone to lay an ambush but still he was feeling far from confident. An almost invisible track led off the road to his left where the three cars had disappeared, and without the fresh tyre tracks he might have missed it altogether. It wound into the low desert hills and there was no indication as to where it might lead.

He listened for several moments but there was no sound to break the stillness of the night, and finally he returned to his car. He was not prepared to follow the mysterious convoy any farther, and after re-starting the engine drove on down the main road. After ten miles he turned on to the hard desert sand and stopped. He relaxed in the front seat but for a long time he remained awake, still thinking and staring up through the windscreen at the star-splashed sky. His thoughts led him nowhere and at last he closed his eyes and slept lightly until dawn.

* * *

He awoke as the first morning rays of the sun warmed him through the windows and sat up stiffly. His water bottle was still full and he soaked his handkerchief to refresh his face, and then he poured a cup of hot coffee from his flask. When he had finished he placed the automatic on the seat beside him once more, started up the car and pulled back on to the road, turning back the way he had come.

He felt reasonably sure that by now the three cars he had followed would have kept to their usual pattern and returned to the villa, but even so he stopped to check for returning tyre tracks before he drove the Mercedes along the vague track into the desert. Low hills and hard stony ground flanked each side, the monotony broken only by scrub bushes and a few rocks. He drove cautiously but there were no signs of life. The sun was becoming hotter, baking the empty wilderness.

The tyre marks that made the track circled behind the hills, shutting the main road out of sight behind him. The Mercedes bumped and swayed in second gear and once Kerim had to grab at his gun as it almost slipped off the seat beside him. Then abruptly he snatched it up again as he was startled by a flurry of movement from a hollow beside the track. A small flock of stray goats scattered and he relaxed and smiled. The goats dispersed, but one more stupid than the rest began to run along the track ahead of him. Kerim watched it, still smiling at his own start of alarm, and then there was a violent explosion and the goat was hurled upwards in a blast of smoke fire and sand, its frightened bleating cut short by abrupt and instantaneous death.

Kerim crashed his foot on the brake and the Mercedes skidded to a halt. The automatic tumbled to the floor and he cursed as he hastily picked it up for the third time. He got out of the car slowly, gazing around the barren landscape, but there was still no sign of life except the surviving goats, now fast disappearing. Kerim's heart was beating noticeably and he walked forward with the automatic in his hand. The sand was settling and the smoke was drifting away from the small crater that had been left in the track. The luckless goat had landed ten yards away, a bloodied and mostly unrecognizable mess. Both of its front legs had been blown off and one of them was completely missing.

Kerim felt a cold sense of anger. He was not a passionate animal lover, but he did not particularly enjoy watching them blown to pieces by booby traps. Judging by the crater he guessed that this one had been some kind of small land mine that had been planted to deal with any prying vehicles like his own. It was sheer luck that the goat had stepped directly on to it. Bad luck for the goat. Good luck for him. Even so he felt angry when he should have been relieved. It was a stupid precaution, and one that was obviously more likely to blow up some innocent shepherd or a stray animal than any genuinely hostile intruder.

He waited for several minutes, again searching the surrounding landscape, but no one came to investigate the explosion. He was puzzled, for at least there should have been someone on hand to tend the goats, but finally he decided to go on. However, the incident had made him even more cautious and he continued on foot, keeping well away from the actual path. He could see now where the previous three cars had circled round the danger spot the night before, but he was not prepared to take any undue risks.

He followed the path round another bend, and then saw that it led into the wide pit of a disused quarry. He approached it warily and saw that the tyre tracks ended in the quarry itself, but still he could see no reason why three car loads of men should come here every night. The whole area was deserted. He guessed that once the quarry had been worked for sand and gravel, but now it was abandoned.

He spent half an hour in searching thoroughly, and by then he was convinced that this was where the mysterious group of men from the villa spent their time between midnight and dawn. He found several cheap cigarette packets, some of them brand new, and there were innumerable fresh footprints in the sand. One of the three cars had leaked a small pool of oil, and he also found some odd scraps of wire and wax wrapping paper. The signs were plentiful, although as yet he could not see how to add them up.

It was the demolished remnants of some small stone huts that gave him his first definite clue. They stood above the quarry and had probably been in use as storehouses or living quarters when the quarry was producing gravel. Now they were heaps of rubble, but Kerim was certain that they had not fallen down but had been blown up. He remembered the bomb trap on the road and carefully re-examined the odd pieces of wire and wax paper that he had picked up. The wire could have been fuse wire, and the paper was the kind that was used to wrap around plastic explosive. With these facts in mind he felt that he was at last getting somewhere, and decided that it was time to leave.

He walked back to the Mercedes, avoiding the dead goat that was already black with hungry flies, and drove thoughtfully back to Damascus.

* * *

He was relieved to find that George was out, presumably touting for tourists, and retiring to his room he caught up on some of his lost sleep. When he awoke in mid-afternoon he washed and shaved quickly and then went out to eat before his host returned. His dislike of the Syrian was growing and he was becoming more and more disgusted with Jackson for placing him with such a repulsive ally. He had realized by now that George was only a very minor fish in the espionage sea, and that Jackson had sent him to Darrasa Street rather than run the risk that a more valuable agent might be compromised by his presence. Which was all very reasonable and security-conscious for Jackson and the rest of his shadowy network, but not exactly reassuring for Kerim.

He finished his meal and by then it was late afternoon. Time for him to get moving again. He did not return to Darrasa Street but instead picked up the Mercedes and drove out towards the quarry once more. He went past the private road to the villa with his foot flat down, and without giving it a glance, but at the same time he made a mental note to return the Mercedes to the car-hire firm and obtain something else. He had used it too often and there was the risk that it would become noticeable.

He reached the road to the quarry before dusk and carried on past it for two or three miles. Then he turned off the road and bumped the car across the hard stony desert until it was out of sight behind the slope of a hill. He climbed out, gathered up his binoculars and the .38 automatic from the dashboard panel

87

and then locked the car. The daylight was fading but he knew that he still had several hours in which to get into position before the occupants of the villa arrived, and he began walking across the desert towards the quarry.

It took him two hours to make the cross-country walk, for he had taken no risk of leaving the car too close. By then it was dark again but the stars were throwing a pale light over the desert. He found the quarry and climbed the barren slope of the nearest sand hill until he reached a clump of prickly thorn that would afford him some concealment. He lay down behind it with the binoculars and the automatic placed close at hand on the hard earth, and then he rolled over on to his back and rested.

An hour passed almost unnoticed. The heavens above him were a fiery glory of hypnotic fascination. He picked out the known star patterns and wondered about those frustratingly distant galaxies. Was there life up there or not? For a while the question dwarfed the mystery he had come to solve and pushed it into the background of his mind. Nothing existed except the universe above him. Then the sound of vehicles approaching in the night brought him reluctantly back to earth.

He turned on to his stomach and raised himself a little to watch the line of headlights growing larger. They stopped short of the quarry and he guessed that the men in the leading car had noticed the dead goat and had disembarked to examine their handiwork. The delay was only a short one and they were obviously satisfied that nothing serious was amiss. The cars came on and drew up in the centre of the quarry.

Kerim used his field glasses and tried to distinguish the faces in the night as the men scrambled out of their cars. There was some form of discipline and he noticed that they all carried weapons, mostly sten guns, as they formed into a group. Two of the men were in charge and giving orders to the rest and Kerim concentrated on these. One was the pock-marked man whom he had decided must be Ahmed Barek. The other was a vigorous, dark-blooded man with black receding hair and a sharp, penetrating voice. He was plainly the senior man present for his authority was never questioned, and he matched the description of the second Egyptian whom Kerim had not previously seen, the elusive Mahmoud Abdel Rashid.

Kerim lay still and observed, and soon his suspicions were proved. Under the direction of the two Egyptians their Syrian pupils moved smartly into a training programme that shattered the peaceful night with small arms fire, the stuttering of stens, and the sharp detonations of plastic explosives. Firing practice and instruction in the ungentle art of sabotage seemed to be the order of the night, and Kerim knew exactly how to fill in the report that Jackson required. The villa was nothing more than a crude school for spies and saboteurs, while this remote and disused quarry served as a practical training ground.

6

Frustration

Kerim lay motionless on his stomach, his elbows braced on the hard ground as he trained his binoculars on the scene below. He had wriggled a little to one side of the thorn bush so that he had an unobstructed view, but he felt reasonably safe from detection. The headlights of the three cars had been switched off, but through the absence of cloud and the brilliance of the stars night was never wholly dark in the desert, and he could distinguish fairly clearly what was taking place. The activity had fast become organized and the Syrian pupils had separated into two groups under their Egyptian teachers. The section under Barek moved away and began setting up targets on the far hillside, while Rashid's section stayed in the quarry.

Kerim concentrated on Rashid and the

group that was listening closely to his words. The Egyptian held something in both hands that was the focal point of their interest, and although Kerim could not define it in the darkness he remembered the wax wrapping paper and was certain that it must be plastic explosive. It was obvious now why the stone huts on the lip of the quarry had been blown up; for Rashid had undoubtedly used them to demonstrate the right amount of explosive that was necessary for their destruction. Now there was nothing left to destroy, and under Rashid's direction the Syrian trainees were simply blasting chunks out of the quarry wall. The sole point of the exercise being to accustom them to the dangerous art of handling the tools of their trade. At a later date he guessed that they would be infiltrated into Israel to cause more practical havoc there.

The noisy clamour of a sten gun made him jump and turn his attention sharply back to the second section under Barek. They had now placed in position a line of three man-sized targets, low on the hillside so that their silhouettes did not stand out too sharply. Barek faced them from a distance of fifty yards with a sten gun cradled in his arms, and as Kerim watched, one of the pupils ran the gauntlet between instructor and target. The young Syrian carried an identical sten gun and was firing wildly from the hip, toppling one of the black-painted targets as he ran. The bullets from Barek's weapon sprayed up sand around his heels and in his haste to get through he missed the remaining targets altogether. The shooting stopped, Barek yelled, and another trainee ran to stand up the target that had fallen. The first man was forced to make the nerve-wracking return trip to rejoin his companions who awaited their own turn, but again he could only topple one target. Barek was making it too hot for him to linger. Kerim winced as the repeated gunfire violated the night, and felt a thin trickle of sweat growing cold along his spine. He was very glad indeed that he had not chosen the wrong hillside from which to keep watch.

There had been no sign of human habitation as he had crossed the desert, and Kerim guessed that the quarry must be well out of the hearing of the nearest village. It was a lonely and isolated spot and ideal for its purpose, for even if the sound of bangs and explosions should be heard they could be dismissed as night-shift blasting for gravel. No one would be likely to hear except a straying peasant such as the one who must have eventually come this morning in search of his lost goats, and the ordinary Arab peasant did not have the intelligence to ask too many questions. And in any case the Syrian authorities must be aware of Rashid's activities, and even if not directly involved would undoubtedly turn a blind eye to cover them up.

His thoughts had become accustomed to the clatter of the sten guns as Barek trained his men in the handling of their weapons under fire, and it was the crack of an explosion from the quarry that next gained Kerim's attention. He saw that Rashid's party had blown another hole out of the quarry wall and were converging to assess the results. The young Syrians were pleased with themselves, but Rashid sounded sharp and angry. Kerim caught some of the words during a lull in Barek's firing practice, and guessed that the explosion had been more powerful than Rashid had demanded. His pupils still had not learned how to judge the right amounts of explosive.

During the next half hour the Egyptian supervised two more detonations, creating clouds of dust and tumbling rocks down on to the quarry floor. By then Kerim decided that he had seen enough and that it was time he made his escape. He had no illusions as to what would happen to him if he were caught and he had no desire to end his career as a bullet-riddled corpse.

He returned his binoculars to their leather case and wrapped the strap around his wrist so that it should not drag. The automatic he pushed into his pocket, for it would be useless against the fire power that could be ranged against him, and then he slowly began to retreat up the slope of the hill. He picked a route that afforded him the most cover, and after every few yards he lay still until he was certain that he had not been seen. He guessed that both Rashid and Barek would approve of a lively man-hunt to brighten up their training programme and his mouth remained obstinately dry until at last he was able to roll over the crest of the hill and slither down through the sand on the far side.

He stood up and brushed the dirt from his clothes, and then began to hurry away. Before him the starlit desert hills were empty and peaceful, but from behind the sound of firearms and the muffled crump of explosions still dominated the night.

★ ★ ★

George was awake when he returned to Darrasa Street, and as he had to pass through the first bedroom to get to his own Kerim could not avoid a conversation with his host. As he entered George switched on the light and sat up in his bed. The young Syrian blinked sleepily and wrinkled the moustache on his upper lip. In the harsh glare of the light his body resembled that of a thin white ferret emerging from the sheets, and Kerim noticed that the chain around his throat supported an old-fashioned locket that hung against his bare chest.

'Kerim,' he seemed surprised. 'I did not expect you to return before dawn. Why did you only stay such a short time today. My mother told me that you came back here to sleep, but left again while I was still out.'

Kerim said calmly, 'I had some business to attend to. Where were you?'

George smiled. 'I met a girl. An English girl. She is travelling with some friends in a Land Rover, but today she was alone. I showed her Damascus, but she has no money. At least, that is what she says. I had to buy her a meal.' His face became sour. 'I took her to my friend's house but she would not make love with me. She is a bitch. I buy her a meal but she will not make love. Some women are like that.'

He stopped and made a grimace of disgust, then said abruptly:

'But what about you? Did you follow the cars from the villa last night? And where have you been tonight?'

Kerim pulled up a chair and sat down, answering the questions as they came.

'Yes I did follow the car, and tonight I was there ahead of them to watch what was happening. Rashid and Barek are using the villa to train saboteurs, no doubt with the intention of sending them into Israel. There's an old quarry out in the desert where they do all the practical stuff. Rashid's the explosives expert. Barek teaches them how to use arms. All I have to do now is to pass my report on to Jackson. Can you make contact for me?'

George nodded. 'Of course, there is a radio.'

'How long will it take?'

George was less certain. 'Perhaps tomorrow.'

Kerim knew from the brief hesitation that George did not know where the radio was. There would be a third party to whom George would have to pass all his reports, and the third man would no doubt pass them on to a fourth who might or might not maintain and operate the radio. George would be the lowest link in the chain, and despite his irritation there was nothing that Kerim could do about it. He said flatly:

'I'll write you out a brief report. Try and get it through tomorrow.'

George nodded and Kerim started to rise, then the Syrian asked:

'Is your mission finished now?'

Kerim paused. 'I hope so. My job was simply to find out whether Rashid and Barek were inside the villa, and if so to find out what they were doing. Now I've found out, and as far as I can see there's not much that Jackson can do about it. The Syrian government must know what's going on, and it's their country. They can allow as many spy schools as they like.'

'So you will be leaving Damascus, that is a pity.' George showed his disappointment. 'I do not like to say goodbye to my friends.'

Kerim made a shrugging movement of his shoulders and moved towards the door. George said hesitantly:

'Do you have to return to your own room?'

Kerim looked back and saw that the young Syrian had moved so that there was room beside him in the bed. He said bluntly:

'Yes, I've got my report to write.'

George's face seemed to contract, his moustache drooping around his mouth. Kerim turned away from him and went into his own room, firmly closing the door. The invitation had not been wholly unexpected and he was glad that he would soon be pulling out. He had seen enough of Damascus.

* * *

The following morning the Syrian newspapers were splashed with dramatic headlines in heavy black print. In a savage air battle over the sea of Galilee Syrian MIG 21 fighters had clashed in dog fights with Israeli jets. The conflict followed a continuous series of exchanges in tank and artillery fire along that particular section of frontier, and the jubilant Syrians claimed five Israeli jets shot down. Kerim later learned that the Arab estimate was exaggerated, but that the Israeli pilots had in fact scored six kills over the Russian-built MIG 21s.

The incident showed a disturbing trend in the increasing hostilities between Israel and her neighbours, and also had an adverse effect upon Kerim's own hopes. If his mission had been marked finished he had planned to return to Cyprus, but when George brought Jackson's reply to his report twenty-four hours later the Major had decided that he should stay on in Damascus. His new instructions were contained inside a sealed envelope and he swore as he read them through.

7467 KERIM SOIRON VIA OPXX4 DAMAS.

REPORT RECEIVED AND UNDERSTOOD. EXCELLENT JOB, BUT NOT IN FULL AGREEMENT YOUR ASSESSMENT OF SITUATION. RECENT ISRAEL-SYRIA ENGAGEMENT CONVINCES ME WAR IMMINENT. BECAUSE OF THIS TRAINING FOR ROUTINE FRONTIER

INFILTRATION SEEMS UNLIKELY. SUS-
PECT SOME MORE DEFINITE OBJECTIVE
INVOLVED. CONTINUE TO OBSERVE AND
REPORT.

J.

George was watching, and awaiting his
response. Kerim had the feeling that
George had probably steamed open the
envelope before delivery, but he gave him
the single sheet of typescript to read.
George studied it wisely and pouted his
underlip, while Kerim crushed the plain
brown envelope in his fist and threw it
angrily to the corner of the room. He
felt frustrated, trapped in a pointless web
that had no meaning.

★ ★ ★

Through George he exchanged the hired
Mercedes for an equally old and dusty
Ford, and once more resumed his daily
vigil on the hillside above the villa. He
did not make any further attempts to
follow the two Egyptians and their Syrian
pupils out to their training ground in the

quarry, for he saw no reason to stick his neck out any farther than was necessary. Once had been enough and he was well aware of how easy it would be for a dozen armed men to hunt him down over the sand hills of the open desert if his presence was to be noticed. It was not a pleasant prospect and he saw no advantage in taking the risk, especially now that he knew what was happening.

For another week he continued to watch the villa, and became even more convinced that he was now wasting his time. The routine of the men inside remained unchanged and he felt that there was nothing more to learn. Even if there was some direct objective behind their training he was unlikely to discover any details by watching from the hillside, and while the guards and dogs patrolled at night there was no opportunity to get into the villa itself. The long hours of observation became dull and monotonous. There were no rewards, the sun was hot, the dust drifted into his throat, and his temper began to deteriorate. He cursed Jackson frequently.

His disillusionment grew gradually, and basically it was because he had too much time in which to think. He thought mostly about Schererzade, wondering whether she was yet able to walk unaided, and whether she still intended to accept Jackson's offer of a job in Israel when her recovery was complete. He knew now that if he had been able to return to Cyprus he would have tried hard to persuade her against such a course, and he wondered whether Jackson had suspected as much. Perhaps that was why Jackson preferred him to waste his time here, skulking in a copse of trees with nothing but the heat and the flies for company.

Schererzade. He tried to picture her again and was annoyed because the memory was blurred. If she went to Israel there might never be an opportunity to strengthen that memory, not unless he was prepared to follow her into Tel Aviv. The thought was bitter, and suddenly he hated Jackson.

It was an exceptionally hot day, he felt sweaty and dirty, and his new trend of thought made him realize that he was becoming weary of the whole stupid merry-go-round of espionage and spying. The money was good, but it was tainted money and sometimes stained with blood. It would be good to get out and live cleanly.

It seemed ironic now that he had started out as an idealist, but that had been under the influence of the C.I.A. In those early years he had firmly believed in the western brand of democracy, and had been fully opposed to the spread of Russian influence that followed the flooding of Soviet arms and ammunitions into the Middle East. Now he was beginning to feel that all politicians and all spy-masters were vultures of the same breed. They cared only for their own positions, their own power and their own sphere of influence, and they were prepared to use any tool or sacrifice any pawn. He was beginning to feel that there was no difference between the conscience of either East or West, and was approaching the philosophy that man was a militant animal forever preying upon his neighbours. Where there was no end there was no goal, and although life would stagnate without conflict he felt that he had contributed his personal share to the endless process.

His idealism had started to diminish even before his exile from Cairo, but after the events that had led him into Morocco on his personal vendetta it had been replaced by a blind hate towards his father's murderers; namely the Egyptian security forces. Now his activities had moved from the Egyptian sphere and that white heat had died. Without the spur of either idealism or hate he had no justification for what he was doing. He had no purpose and had become a pawn under Jackson's direction. His father had been French, his mother Arab, and his paymasters American and British. He had no true home and no roots. He was beginning to tire.

After that first week he received another communication from Jackson, passed as before through the chain of the unknown radio operator and George. Jackson had decided that a photographic record of Rashid, Barek and all their Syrian pupils could be useful, and so Kerim spent the next few days in lurking above the villa with a camera instead of binoculars. He had fitted a high-powered telescopic lens, and after three days had managed to snap front face pictures of most of the Syrians as they relaxed on the lawns during the late afternoons. On the third day he also managed to get Barek's dark, pock-marked features into focus, but Rashid continued to elude him. The senior of the two Egyptians rarely showed his face outside the villa and when he did it was only briefly. However, the task gave Kerim something to do, and kept his mind from his brooding thoughts.

To complete the record he took extensive photographs of the villa and its grounds, but another two days passed before he was able to add Rashid to his list. On that day he had taken up his position on the hillside at noon, for he had long since given up the watch during the morning when he knew that the occupants of the villa would only sleep. There was usually no activity until after three o'clock and so he relaxed in his hiding place among the concealing oak trees. He heard a few cars or lorries go past on the main road, and then unexpectedly he heard the sound of a car moving in the villa grounds.

He sat up and saw that one of the three cars that were kept garaged behind the villa had been driven round to the front by the verandah. The car had made afternoon trips before, presumably into Damascus to buy supplies, and at first Kerim saw nothing unusual. Then Rashid appeared on the verandah.

The Egyptian was wearing a smartly cut black suit, and carried both a small suitcase and a briefcase, and it was obvious that he was leaving. He stopped before getting into the car and it seemed that the whole school had followed him out. Hands were shaken all round, and finally Rashid paused for a longer handshake and some parting words with Barek. Kerim abruptly remembered his camera and there was just sufficient time for him to focus and take his picture before Rashid turned and got into the car. The Egyptian relaxed in the back seat and then the car moved off. The iron gates were pulled open and several of the young Syrians were still waving a cheerful farewell as the car drove out of the grounds.

Kerim swapped his camera for his binoculars and watched the car as it turned on to the main road and gathered speed in the direction of Damascus. A cloud of white dust soon blotted it from view, and Kerim could only curse the fact that his own car was not at hand to enable him to follow it. George would not arrive with the car to pick him up until much later in the evening, and again he felt that his presence here was useless. He could do nothing but watch and wait until the car from the villa returned a little over an hour later, and note that Rashid was no longer in the back seat. The driver had returned alone.

7

Jerusalem

Kerim reported Rashid's departure, but for two more infuriating days he was obliged to keep up his observations on the villa. The routine of its occupants remained unchanged, except that Barek was now clearly in charge, with the most efficient of the young Syrians promoted to his second in command. Rashid did not return, and the fact that he had not been in a position to follow the Egyptian to his unknown destination made Kerim positive that he was wasting his time. And then Jackson called him off and instructed him to fly to Amman.

Kerim read the radio message with a mixture of relief and irritation. He wanted to leave Damascus but he did not particularly want to go to Amman. Also Jackson had stressed that he take the next flight when his reception would be arranged at Amman airport, which gave him only a matter of hours to pack up and leave. After weeks of hanging about everything now had to be done in a rush.

He telephoned the airport to reserve his seat, and then George helped him to pack. Nothing had happened to lessen his dislike for the young Syrian, but from George's viewpoint they were still friends and it was an unhappy parting. Kerim shook hands briefly, refused to kiss him, and left Darrasa Street as quickly as he could.

A taxi took him to the airport and there he had an hour to wait before boarding his plane to Amman. It was a short flight of less than an hour, with nothing but desert and a few small villages passing below. It seemed to Kerim that he had hardly settled and made himself comfortable before they were landing again. The customs and passport controls delayed him, but there was no restriction on travellers between Syria and Jordan and his Lebanese passport was considered friendly. He picked up his suitcase and walked clear of the controls, stopping at the bank exchange desk to transfer his Syrian currency into Jordanian dinars. When the transaction was completed he moved away and then stopped again to check through the handful of crisp new notes, waiting to be approached.

There was no sign of anybody being on hand to meet him.

He spent a minute in placing the money into his wallet, separating the notes into different compartments according to their value. Then he returned the wallet to his pocket, picked up his suitcase again and walked calmly out of the airport. His instructions had specified that he must arrive on this flight, but there was no one to meet him. Presumably something had gone wrong, most likely a mere technical hitch, but he was not taking the risk of waiting around.

He allowed a moment of grace as he came out of the airport building, stopping to put on his dark sunglasses as he stepped out into the fierce glare, but still no one approached him. He called a taxi and told the driver to take him into the city.

It was a distance of two and a half miles into the city centre, and after the first mile Kerim had placed the car that had appeared to follow him. He had shifted into the corner of the taxi so that he could see the rear view mirror over the driver's shoulder, and the tailing car had appeared after the first five minutes. It was a large black American sedan.

Kerim began to sweat a little. His cameras had again aroused no suspicions when he had declared them at the airport, but the photographs that he had taken at the villa were in the lining of his suitcase and those were incriminating. And even more incriminating was the .38 automatic which lay flat against the small of his back beneath the waistband of his trousers. A really determined search could not fail to nail him.

His driver asked for more explicit instructions as they entered the heart of the city, and Kerim told him to stop at a reasonable hotel. The man obeyed, and Kerim was aware that the big American car had pulled into the kerb fifty yards behind as he paid his fare. The taxi moved off and Kerim turned towards the hotel, not hurrying but walking as quickly as he dared. A row of parked cars had forced the taxi to pull up short and leave him a twenty yard walk, but if he could reach the hotel then there was a chance that he could smartly exit through a side door and get clear.

He heard the big American car moving up behind him.

He turned in towards the hotel entrance, and in the same moment the car that had been parked directly in front of the hotel moved away. The black sedan slipped smoothly into the vacant space and stopped. Kerim saw its reflection in the glass front of the hotel doorway but did not look round. He was on the steps when a voice hailed him.

'Welcome to Jordan. Care for a lift.'

Kerim turned on his heel, recognized the speaker, and shut his mouth on a curse of exasperation. He turned back across the pavement to the black car and got inside. He pushed his suitcase into the back and while he did so the car nosed out into the traffic stream once more.

Williamson, usually called Bill, said calmly:

'Sorry you had to fork out the price of a taxi, but it's a bit dodgy to meet you actually at the airport. Too many eyes watching; theirs, ours, everybody elses. Much better to watch for the taxies coming out of the airport, and then follow you into the city.'

Kerim said sourly, 'Someone might have warned me.'

Williamson grinned. 'I can appreciate your point, but it's a recent procedure. Just lately the airports in this part of the world have become more like international clubs for secret agents. Everybody watches everybody else. We're thinking of issuing them all with old school ties to simplify recognition, then we'll be able to hold social evenings and reunion parties.'

'Count me out.' Kerim watched as Williamson smoothly accelerated past a battered lorry, and then asked, 'But just as a matter of interest, what are you doing in Amman? Or would that be breaking security?'

'Not to you it wouldn't. I'm working with the Major. Co-ordinating reports and so forth. All desk work and a bit dreary really. It makes a nice change to come out into the daylight for five minutes. The Major sent me because we've met before.'

As he spoke Williamson turned the car into a small, underground park that served an almost modern, five-storied block of offices. Pale electric light replaced the hot sun as they dipped down the ramp into the park, and Williamson stopped the car close against the far wall. Kerim waited while he switched off the ignition, and then said:

'What exactly does Jackson want from me?'

Williamson smiled cheerfully. 'Let's go and ask him. I think he's waiting.'

Kerim shrugged and got out of the car. He waited while Williamson locked the doors and then followed the young Englishman up a flight of concrete steps that brought them on to the ground floor of the office building. A lift conveyed them up to the fifth floor. They were the only passengers and Williamson operated the buttons. Then he led the way along a short corridor and stopped in front of a door that bore a single square pane of pebbled glass. Across the glass were the gold-painted words:

K. L. MAZHAR. AIR FREIGHT & EXPORTS LTD.

Williamson knocked and went in.

Kerim followed him and briefly noticed the routine office interior. There was a chair for visitors and a desk-counter littered with sales literature advertising various airlines. A young woman sat typing behind the counter, but after recognizing Williamson paid no more attention as the young Englishman crossed to a door marked PRIVATE. He nodded to an elderly man who sat behind another desk in the more comfortable inner office, and then carried on through yet another door. Here, in the final sanctum, Jackson arose from behind the most disorderly arrayed desk of all to greet them. The Major was casually dressed in grey trousers and a checked-patterned shirt with the sleeves rolled up above the wrists. He looked untidy compared to Williamson's quiet brown business suit and Kerim's own neatly tailored grey, but he did not appear to notice. The blue eyes were a little tired but his grip was still hard and British.

'Hello, Soiron. I see Bill picked you up all right. How was the trip?'

'Rushed,' Kerim answered. He looked around the cramped room with its cheap, overcrowded appearance and said:

'According to the movies this place should be ten times as large, all glass and chromium, and fancy dials and gadgets. Invincible and unreachable. What went wrong?'

Jackson grinned. 'Movie producers get a damned sight better budget to work with than I do. If the War Office suspected there was an electric toaster in here I'd be cashiered for misappropriating funds. If I was handsome I'd quit and be a film star.'

There were two straight-backed chairs facing Jackson's desk. Williamson relaxed in one, and after a moment Kerim occupied the other. The Major sat down again, pushed one hand through his sand-coloured hair to smooth it back across his head, and then he began to talk.

'No doubt the first thing you want to know is why you're here.' He smiled briefly. 'The answer is very simple. Your missing friend Rashid came to Jordan. We spotted him at Damascus airport, even before your report came through that he had left the villa. He boarded an SAS flight for Amman and we picked him up again when he landed here. I had a man on hand to follow him and he was tailed to the Intercontinental Hotel here in the city. He didn't stay there but spent a couple of hours in conference with three un-named men in a private suite. He left very late in the evening, got into a car and was driven away. My man was positioned to follow in another vehicle and the trail led him to Jerusalem. Unfortunately he had to stay well back on the open road across the desert, and he left it a little too late in closing the gap. The car carrying Rashid vanished somewhere in Jerusalem, and my man lost contact. We haven't been able to trace him since.'

Kerim said bluntly, 'You sound well-organized. It shouldn't be too difficult to find him again.'

Jackson's smile became a little rueful. 'We are well organized at the airports, but it doesn't extend much farther. That's why I need you again, I want you to go into Jerusalem and find Rashid for me. I've got a hunch that our Egyptian friend is up to some more mischief, and if we can find him it should prove profitable to keep a continued watch on his movements. He has already organized this spy school in Syria, and now that he's moved on and left Barek in charge I think it not unlikely that he might be doing something similar here in Jordan. If he is then I want to know all about it.'

Kerim could feel the endless merry-go-round starting up again. He said wearily:

'Is it really worth it? If Rashid is setting

up another spy school, and training more saboteurs and infiltrators, then there is nothing that can be done about it. You can warn the Israelies, but I think that they are capable of taking care of these people when they appear on the frontier. What do you gain?'

Jackson stared at him. 'You surprise me. In this business we have to try and know everything. It's true that a lot of useless information does accumulate, including facts where on the face of it we can't do much about them anyway. But we still have to try and know everything, otherwise some of the really vital items might escape our notice. Especially at a time like this when the whole of the Middle East is moving into another holy bloodbath. Syria, Jordan and Egypt are becoming more and more aggressive. There are a dozen Arab radio stations blaring out endless streams of abuse and incentive to war against the Israelies. That dog fight over Galilee was only a beginning. The pot's boiling and the lid has to blow sky-high. It's only a matter of time.'

He paused, relaxing a little, and then said:

'But to get back to this particular business of Rashid. I'm not satisfied that it is as simple as it appears on the surface. Training infiltrators is a general answer, and I want something more exact. What is the end result? What is the target? That's what I want to know.'

Kerim said calmly, 'What's wrong with the usual targets; military installations, air fields, oil supplies. They'll be sent in before war is declared.'

Jackson nodded. 'You're probably right. But I can't make an accurate guess and leave it at that. I have to be sure.'

Kerim was silent for a moment, and then he said:

'All right, I'll go into Jerusalem on one condition.'

'What's that?'

'That you don't ask me to work with another blasted pouf.'

Jackson leaned back and chuckled. 'Sorry about that. But don't be too hard on George. This is supposed to be an understanding age, and he does have his uses.'

'I failed to see them.'

'Well for a start he dredges up a few oddments of information now and again. He moves about a lot, and he knows most of the rif-raf in Damascus.' The Major moved forward once more and added seriously, 'But his main value in this case was that he was dispensable. I told you that if anything went wrong I could have shifted you out of Syria pretty sharpish. George would have been nominated for the chop. You had to play a lone hand anyway, all you needed was a place to stay and a weak link with me. George provided both.'

Kerim was not wholly appeased and asked a little bitterly:

'So what kind of a dispensable weak link have you arranged for me this time?'

'None, you can stay at a hotel. Jerusalem is still full of tourists so you won't be out of place with your cameras. If you have anything to report you can make a telephone call direct to me. Ask for mister Aziz Mazhar. There isn't such a gentleman, but you'll be put through and I'll tell you that you'll have to call back. Then I'll send Bill down to see you. Jerusalem is only seventy miles from here by road.'

Kerim affirmed that he understood, and then Jackson went on to question him more closely about his observations of the Syrian spy school. There was little that he could add to his radioed reports, but eventually he produced the photographs that were hidden in his suitcase. There had been time to develop and blow up the prints during his idle mornings in Damascus, using a darkroom owned by a friend of George, and now the two Englishmen leaned closer as he spread the collection of dark Syrian faces over the desk. Jackson paused over the pock-marked face of Barek, and then picked out the picture of Rashid. It was not a perfect photograph, but it showed clearly enough the swarthy Egyptian face with the receding black hair and the slightly distended nostrils of the large nose. Jackson tapped it with his thumb and expressed his satisfaction.

'This should be useful. Now that we can circulate copies with his description we might be able to find out something definite about him.'

There seemed to be nothing more to discuss, but Kerim hesitated as he closed up his suitcase. There was a question that he wanted to ask and now seemed as good a time as any. Finally he said:

'Is there any news from Cyprus?'

Jackson looked puzzled, then enlightenment came.

'You mean Schererzade. She was discharged from the hospital in Nicosia two days ago. She's already made her application to the Israeli Embassy, and I don't think there'll be any hitch about getting her into Tel Aviv. Everything is working out nicely.'

Kerim said nothing, and tried to hide the tight anger that had knotted in his stomach.

* * *

He spent the night in Amman, and then boarded a bus for Jerusalem the following morning. The bus was late in starting and slow in climbing up the steep roads out of the capital. Kerim looked back and was unimpressed. Amman was nothing more than a great sprawl of untidy concrete buildings filling up a huge bowl in the hills, and he was not sorry to be leaving. The journey was long, hot, dusty and tiring, and he was relieved when at last the bus entered Jerusalem.

The road passed between the Mount of Olives and the Garden of Gethsemane on the one side, and part of the ancient, time-mellowed walls of the old city on the other. Beyond the wall rose the great golden dome of the magnificent octagonal mosque that was built above the bare rock that Abraham had intended as the altar for the sacrifice of his son to God. The Dome Of The Rock was sacred to Islamic faith, and within the same city walls rose the Church of the Holy Sepulchre, built upon the site of the crucifixion, resurrection and burial of Christ. They were only two of the holy places of Jerusalem, the city sacred to Moslem, Christian and Jew.

Kerim was not a religious man, but neither was he agnostic. He did not pretend to know the nature of God, but he knew that God could not belong to any one religion alone. He could sense the soul and spirit of Jerusalem in the old walls and narrow streets, flanked by the hills and olive groves that had remained dusty and changeless through the centuries. Something was stirred inside him, and from the first view it was not apparent that the ancient ramparts on the west side of the old city formed the barrier between Israel and Jordan, between Arab and Jew. A wall of hate as solid and detestable as that which divided Berlin.

That was not immediately obvious. The first impression was that of age and peace and sun-soaked simplicity. And as Kerim descended from the bus and called a taxi to find him a hotel, he felt the taste of disgust in his own presence here.

8

The Convent

The Petra Hotel was situated close to the west wall, only a stone's throw from the massive, squared bastion of David's Tower. From its flat roof it was possible to look over the walls into the forbidden half of Israeli Jerusalem, while to the east the view extended over the whole of the old city to the Mount of Olives beyond. The hotel was neither too grand nor too small and suited Kerim's requirements perfectly. He booked a single room, made himself comfortable, and proceeded to make himself familiar with the city.

He followed his normal procedure of working hard at his freelance photography. The well-illustrated articles he had prepared in Damascus he despatched to various Lebanese, French and American magazines, replacing them with new material photographed in and around

Jerusalem. The Holy city was an endless treasure house of ideas and subjects, but as he roamed with his cameras he did not forget that his basic purpose was to find Rashid. He listened to the talk in the cafés and bazaars, and was continually alert for any glimpse of the dark Egyptian face with the receding hair.

After a week he had built up enough evidence to protect his cover, and began to concentrate more fully on his search. He was rarely in his hotel except to sleep. He took his meals in the cheap eating places in and around the bazaar, listening to the chatter of voices around him and drinking endless cups of coffee. Finally he was certain that Rashid was not in Jerusalem itself, at least, not in Jordanian Jerusalem, but that was no more than he had expected.

He hired a car, a Volkswagen 1200 saloon, and began to venture farther afield. He made innocent trips, south to Bethlehem and Hebron, north to Nablus and Sebastya, and east to Jericho. All were on the tourist intinerary, for in all these places Jesus Christ had walked and taught and healed. Kerim Soiron conscientiously visited all the holy places, but they were only a valid excuse to drive along the roads leading out of Jerusalem. He was searching for another walled villa similar to the Syrian spy school outside Damascus, for if Jackson was right and Rashid was engaged in organizing an identical school, then he would have to have another base. Kerim reasoned that it should be easier to locate the base than the man.

He marked down several possible locations during his travels, paying attention to any large building that was sufficiently isolated, but gradually he was able to eliminate them all from his list. There were many roadside stalls selling water melons or soft drinks where he could stop and make casual conversation about the surrounding areas, and the proprietors were usually well-informed and prepared to gossip in the hope of lengthening a customer's stay. A few well placed enquiries in the general talk served to clear each possibility in turn, satisfying him that the owners were innocent and long established in the neighbourhood.

He was prepared to report failure, and was personally of the opinion that Rashid had either returned to Amman or vanished to new pastures. Then, unexpectedly, chance made one of its rare interventions to repay his perseverance. He was returning from one of his excursions along the north road when he passed two husky young Arabs taking down a sign by a narrow side road. The two men were stripped to the waist and worked with a capable efficiency of movement that was not normally noticeable among Arab workmen. Instinct sharpened Kerim's attention and he looked back to read the words on the sign as it was lowered to the ground. It said simply:

THE ST MAGDALENE CONVENT
FOR YOUNG LADIES

Kerim drove slowly and thoughtfully without looking back, but several tiny factors began to add up in his mind. One was that the sign had been in good repair and that there was no logical reason to take it away. Two was that workmen employed by a convent for young ladies would hardly be likely to go about their duties bare to the waist. And three was that although the convent had not been visible from the road it was almost certain to be large, isolated and well protected. Added together those seemingly minor points made a question mark that demanded at least a cursory investigation.

He stopped the Volkswagen after another half mile, parking beside one of the roadside stalls he had frequented so often during the past week. Here he ordered a cold drink, an endless necessity in the dusty heat, and drank it gratefully. He was served by a young Arab boy, and when he replaced the empty bottle and paid he casually asked for directions to the St Magdalene Convent. The boy shrugged his thin shoulders and pointed back along the road, speaking in Arabic.

'It is that way, perhaps a kilometre. But it is not a convent any more. The nuns have left many weeks ago.'

Kerim looked surprised. 'You mean it is empty? It was recommended to me in Jerusalem as a suitable school for my younger sister.'

The boy shrugged again. 'It is not empty. There are new people there. Strangers. For a month they have been at the convent, but I do not know what they do. They are not friendly. Now it is not a good place for anybody's sister.'

The words were a solemn warning, and an invitation for further questions which Kerim declined. He could sense that the boy was eager to gossip, but he had learned enough and simply remarked that he would enquire in Jerusalem for another school. He added his thanks and went back to his car, driving off without a backward glance towards the city.

★ ★ ★

He returned later in the evening when the light was fading and the yellow hills were turning gold against the setting sun. The air was still warm and the eastern sky was a darkening blue. He drove slowly past the spot where the two men had been dismantling the sign, but now both the men and the signpost had gone. There was just the empty roadway quickly losing itself in the hills.

He continued driving until he passed a grove of ancient olive trees behind which he could park the Volkswagen out of sight of the main road, then he walked back. He turned off on to the hard white path of the private roadway and followed it as it twisted upwards. It was dusk now but he moved carefully, ready to dive for cover behind the neat line of dark green cypress trees that lined the road. However, nothing alarmed him and he reached the highest point of the path where it turned down again between the hills. The soft shadows were becoming darker and in the far distance he could hear the tinkle of a goat's bell. Below him the road dipped down into a small, shallow valley filled with orange and lemon groves, and on the far slope stood a solid, grey-walled building that could only be the convent.

Kerim hurried quickly down the slope,

anxious to get below the skyline. He stopped where a clump of scrub threw a patch of black shadow and knelt there to study his surroundings. He noted that the encircling hills were bare, with no useful copses of trees where he might be able to observe in daylight. The floor of the valley below was flat, and in the poor light the close, dark-leaved groves of small orange and lemon trees looked almost like a black lake. The convent he studied last of all, using a new pair of binoculars that Jackson had provided for him before he left Amman. The building was squared and sombre, with two wings embracing a small, cobbled courtyard. Heavy, iron-barred gates sealed it from the outside world, and with its sloping, grey-tiled roofs and a marked infrequency of windows it reminded him of a prison. There were lights showing inside, but he could see no other signs of activity and decided to move closer.

It took him fifteen minutes to descend the hill and move through the groves of young trees to approach the convent, and by then the night was as dark as the starry desert sky would allow. He stopped when he could overlook the last fifty yards of open ground before the convent, for on the slope of the hill outside the bleak stone walls the earth had been carefully cultivated into flower gardens and vegetable plots. On the edge of the lemon grove he lay down upon his stomach and used his binoculars once more.

He could see through the closed bars of the gateway into the courtyard. It was dimly lighted and there he could see an ancient olive tree planted in the centre of the cobblestones to give shade. Something white fluttered from the gnarled and wide-spread branches. Kerim focused more clearly and recognized a line of washed clothes, mostly of feminine underthings. It gave him a jolt of disappointment and he wondered if his suspicions could be wrong. There had been no women in the villa at Damascus and he had expected none here.

However, he waited, hoping to catch a glimpse of the convent's new occupants. There was no sign of a guard on the gate, which again made him dubious, but he wanted to be sure that he was wrong before he turned away. For thirty minutes he lay in the lemon grove and nothing stirred within the convent walls. Then a woman appeared and began to take down the line of underclothes.

Kerim studied her closely. She was young but not particularly attractive, there was something hard and slightly masculine about her movements. She had Arab blood, her hair was black and long, and she wore a plain brown dress. A man appeared as she finished her task. He spoke to her and it looked as though he had offered to carry her basket. The girl smiled but shook her head, and carried the basket of washing past him into the convent. The man smiled at her retreating back, a broad, sensuous smile that could have made his face ugly to some women yet attractive to others. It was a familiar face with a broad nose and the obvious Arab blood. It was the face of Mahmoud Abdel Rashid.

A feeling of quiet elation pulsed through Kerim's veins, and he too allowed himself a slow smile.

He backed off and returned to his car.

★ ★ ★

It was the beginning of more long, dreary weeks of routine observation, but this time there were more difficulties and Kerim liked the job even less. He could not watch from a safe distance for there was no concealment on the bare hills, which meant that he had to watch from the lemon groves immediately below the convent, arriving before dawn and lying in hiding throughout the day until darkness again covered his retreat. He made certain that there were no dogs or gardeners before risking a daytime watch, but even so it was uncomfortable and dangerous. He preferred to watch at night.

He was able to establish over a period of time that the convent had twelve occupants other than Rashid. There were nine men and three women, but the women looked as fit and capable as the men and Kerim no longer had any doubts that he had found another spy school. The fact that there had been no women at the Syrian school became irrelevant, for women had been used for espionage many times before and it should not have surprised him that it was happening again.

He built up another photographic dossier on these new recruits, but this time it took him much longer. He could not overlook the convent as he had overlooked the villa outside Damascus, and could only aim the telescopic lens of his camera at the small section of courtyard visible through the closed bars of the gate. Consequently the vertical lines of the bars partially obscured every print. It was annoying but it was the best he could do, for the convent remained a sealed community. There were no midnight training expeditions, and only twice a week did a car leave the convent to drive into Jerusalem, presumably for supplies.

Kerim had called the Amman telephone number of K. L. Mazhar, Air Freight & Exports, immediately after he had located the convent. Bill Williamson had appeared the following day to listen to his report, and since then the young Englishman had contacted him every seven days, usually by following him from the Petra Hotel and then making himself known in the crowded anonymity of the bazaars. After a month Williamson brought a request from Jackson for a complete list of names, histories, backgrounds, characteristics and vices to match up with the photographs of the spy school students; plus details of Rashid's exact intentions. Kerim greeted the request with disgusted laughter and replied that it was impossible. Two days later Williamson appeared again, falling casually into step beside him a few minutes after he had left his hotel, and suggesting a small café where they could talk. Kerim sensed trouble, and was not surprised when he ducked through the low, arched entrance to the café and found Jackson waiting at a corner table.

The Major wore a casual grey shirt and trousers, and had treated his sandy hair with a black dye to make it less noticeable. However, his tough, creased face was fitted with the usual friendly grin which Kerim had learned to distrust. They exchanged informal remarks while coffee was brought to their table, but when they were alone Jackson wasted no time in getting down to business. Kerim answered the searching questions, repeating the facts of his earlier reports, and waited for the attack. It came, sugared with a faint coating of praise. Jackson said grimly:

'You've done a nice job, Kerim. Both in finding Rashid, and in covering the convent. But it's not enough. We still know no more about Rashid's exact intentions than we did before he vanished from Damascus. We anticipated that he would be setting up another spy school here in Jerusalem, and now that we've found it we have to know why. Somehow you've got to infiltrate into that spy school.'

Kerim said flatly, 'It's not possible. It was built to keep intruders out, and even if I could get inside the odds are that I would be dead or a prisoner in a matter of minutes. You're asking too much.'

'All right, if you can't get into the convent you'll have to try and get at one of the students. Try a bribe, there are not many Arabs who wouldn't sell out their own mothers for a fistful of hard cash. And if that fails you can always try blackmail. Where you've got more than a couple of Arabs together you've usually got a few homosexuals. They're always a good target.'

Kerim's mouth tightened, for Jackson was forgetting that he too was part Arab. He said coldly:

'It is a mistake to underestimate your opponents, Major, even if they are Arabs. But in any case it is still not possible to do what you want. These people stay inside the convent. There are no opportunities to approach them. You cannot bribe or blackmail a man from a distance of fifty yards when you are hiding like a thief in a lemon grove.'

'There must be opportunities,' Jackson insisted. 'What about these twice-weekly trips into Jerusalem to buy food supplies? Who drives the car?'

142

'One of the girl students.'

'She goes alone?'

'Yes. They probably think that one woman on her own is less noticeable. A shopping expedition is a woman's job.'

'True, but it's rather foolish of them not to send a man to cover her.'

Jackson tugged thoughtfully at his jaw, and then said more quietly, 'Perhaps it's unnecessary to think in terms of bribery and blackmail. It's not really British anyway. Good, old-fashioned normal sex should do just as well.'

'Meaning what exactly?'

Jackson smiled. 'Meaning that you're quite a handsome young man. You should be able to charm a few secrets out of a girl.'

Kerim said angrily, 'Perhaps I can, but it's not the kind of job I want. Why not employ Bill to do your dirty work. He has a certain British charm.'

Williamson grinned hastily. 'Not me, old boy. Arab girls are not quite my style.'

There was an awkward silence, and then Jackson said:

'Even if they were, Bill, you're still not suitable for this job. An Englishman would make the girl too suspicious. But you, Kerim, you're part Arab. You should be able to do it. Make a casual contact. Get talking to her. Find out what her sympathies are and agree with everything she says. Be pro-Arab, anti-Israel, kill the Jews, three cheers for Nasser — be anything that you have to be to win her confidence. If you can't get into the convent and none of the other inhabitants come out then she's the only line of approach we have.'

He paused, and then went on even more seriously:

'I've explained before why it is so important that we find out exactly what Rashid intends to do. The Middle East situation speaks for itself and I shouldn't have to explain it again.'

Kerim said nothing for a moment. Jackson's words were a sop for his conscience and his pride, but there was the faint glimmer of a threat in the Major's hard blue eyes. Agents who failed to obey orders didn't get paid. And what was worse they became an embarrassment that would eventually have to be removed. Kerim knew all the rules only too well. He said at last:

'All right, I'll do my best to work through the girl. But I don't promise anything.'

Jackson smiled and said cheerfully:

'Fine! I expected no less. We'll have another cup of coffee and then Bill and I will have to get back to Amman. Use the same telephone routine if you should have anything to report, otherwise Bill will just pop up from time to time to see how you're getting on.'

Kerim nodded. Jackson paid for the coffee but to Kerim it tasted sour.

9

Dalia

A few mornings later the girl drove the convent car into the walled area of the old city of Jerusalem. She stopped the car on the edge of the bazaar area, locked it securely, and then vanished into one of the dark, crowded lanes with a large shopping bag on her arm. Three times she reappeared to unload her purchases into the boot of the car, and after the third trip she returned to the driving seat. She switched on the ignition, pressed the starter and heard the electric motor whir. The engine did not start.

The girl made two more attempts, tightened her lips and then got out of the car. She was young, in her early twenties, and her expression was of resigned annoyance. She wore a simple blue dress, flat-soled sandals on her feet, and a bright coloured scarf around her dark hair. She

146

opened up the bonnet of the car with a sharp angry movement and peered inside. From behind her a friendly voice asked:

'Is anything wrong? Perhaps I can help?'

She turned to meet a pair of steel sharp, but smiling grey eyes. The words had been spoken in Arabic, the tone polite and not too forward. The man was casually dressed, his face neither light nor dark and strangely ageless. He could have been twenty-five or in his late thirties, but it was impossible to define. The girl regarded him for a moment and then said:

'This stupid car will not start.'

Kerim smiled and she moved to one side so that he could examine the engine. He tugged knowledgeably at the sparking plug leads to check that they were tight, frowning and proding thoughtfully. At the same time he was careful not to touch the high tension lead to the coil which he had wrenched loose ten minutes earlier. The lead was still in position but the contact was broken. Finally he looked up and said:

'Try it now.'

The girl returned to the car and pressed the starter several times in succession. Again without result. She got out of the car again and watched while he tinkered a little further, removing the distributor cap and dubiously examining the contact points and rotor arm. Finally he replaced the cap and suggested that she try a third time. Still there was no result. Kerim leaned close to the driving window and said apologetically:

'I'm sorry, but I've tried everything I can think of. All that I can do now is to offer you a tow to a garage. I have my own car parked about a hundred yards away.'

The girl hesitated, and stared at him hard for a moment. Then she managed a slightly strained smile.

'Thank you very much. I will accept your offer.'

Kerim smiled in return and then slammed down the bonnet of her car. The last thing he wanted was for some even more helpful by-passer to repair the car in his absence, and so he lost no time in fetching his own car to the spot. He had exchanged the Volkswagen in case it had become too familiar, and was now driving a small Fiat saloon.

It took him half an hour to fasten a rope and tow the stranded car with the girl inside to a garage. There an Arab mechanic regarded it doubtfully and indicated that his time was already fully booked with waiting repair jobs. Kerim had deliberately picked a garage which he knew to be busy, and he judged his time carefully before interrupting the argument that ensued. He did not want to appear too eager, but if the mechanic were persuaded to make a preliminary examination on the spot he would be too late. He chose his moment and said:

'If it will help, perhaps you will permit me to drive you home, or wherever it is that you wish to go. Then you can return tomorrow to collect your car. Twenty-four hours should give them time to find out what is wrong with the engine.'

The mechanic nodded cheerfully.

'By tomorrow yes, but today is impossible.'

This time the girl's hesitation was longer. Kerim's offer had given the mechanic increased hopes of escaping a rushed job, and she knew that he would be even more difficult. Kerim sensed that she had become wary, and wondered if her suspicions were aroused. Perhaps Rashid had expressly warned her against any approach by strangers. He waited, not daring to press his offer too hard, and then the girl looked at him and reluctantly nodded.

'All right, if you will take me home I will leave the car until tomorrow. It is good of you to go to such trouble.'

Kerim smiled. 'It is a pleasure.'

She left the supplies that had been the cause of her journey in the boot of her own car, but Kerim made no comment. He was not supposed to know what she had been doing. She seated herself in the Fiat beside him and her manner was still a little reserved. Kerim did not try to break that reserve down too quickly as they drove out of Jerusalem, and did not make the mistake of turning along the north road until she directed him to do so.

The girl was silent for the first few miles, gazing out at the rolling yellow hills. Then gradually she became more friendly and asked him who he was, and what was his business in Jerusalem. Kerim gave her his name, and invited her to look through some of his photographs which were in the front of the car. They were all glossy prints of the holy places and he explained his journalistic cover. His cameras were in evidence on the back seat of the car, although without the special telescopic lens. He thanked her when she commented politely on the quality of his pictures, and then looked at her directly and said:

'But you have not yet told me your name?'

She smiled. 'It is Dalia.'

When she smiled she was not unattractive, and Kerim was almost serious when he said:

'A pretty name for a pretty girl. Perhaps I can take your photograph sometime?'

She shook her head. 'It is not possible. I am sorry.'

Her tone was sincere, and the ice appeared to be broken between them. Dalia continued to converse, mostly in general terms about his work, and Kerim began to relax. They were approaching the side road that led to the convent and automatically his right foot began to shift towards the brake pedal. Dalia was watching his face and asking how long he would be staying in Jordan, and then abruptly he saw the mistake that he had almost made. His expression did not change as he answered that as yet he had set no limit upon the length of his stay, but he increased pressure on the accelerator once more and they sped past the opening. Dalia glanced back and said quickly:

'I am sorry. We should have stopped back there. I forgot to tell you.'

Kerim slowed the car and looked back over his shoulder.

'That's all right,' he said calmly. 'I can turn around.'

They exchanged smiles, and Dalia

looked just a little embarrassed. Kerim wondered whether she had been deliberately trying to trap him, and if so whether she had noticed that fractional decrease in speed a moment before she had told him to stop. He couldn't be sure on either point.

He reversed the car and drove back to the side turning, but as he swung off the road she again told him to stop. He did so and she said:

'Thank you very much, but from here I can walk.'

'Walk to where?'

She smiled. 'There is a convent school just over those hills. That is where I am going.'

'Then I'll drive you the rest of the way.'

She touched his arm. 'No, Kerim. I told you, it is a convent school. They will not approve if I return with a strange man. I will walk and tell them that I came back from Jerusalem by bus along the main road.'

Kerim hesitated, but he did not press her any farther. She got out of the car and raised her hand in farewell, and then he asked hopefully:

'Dalia, is it possible that I can see you again?'

She shook her head. 'No, Kerim. It is not possible. But again I thank you very much for bringing me home.'

She turned and began to walk briskly along the dusty unmade road. Kerim watched, and then he backed the car out on to the main road again and drove back into Jerusalem.

* * *

The following morning when she came to collect her car Kerim was waiting. He had half feared that one of the male students would be sent in her place and allowed himself a smile as he saw her enter the garage. While she was talking to the mechanic he had time to assure himself that no third party was also watching her movements, and as she drove out of the garage forecourt and halted on the roadside he spoke casually through the open driving window.

154

'Good morning, Miss Dalia. I'm pleased to see that your car has been repaired. What was the trouble?'

She was startled by his voice, and recognition brought a fleeting smile followed by sharp suspicion.

'Good morning, Kerim. The garage man says that the high tension lead was loose, whatever that may mean, but at least it was not very expensive.' She gazed at him coolly. 'But why are you here? I do not believe in coincidence.'

'That's wise, and this isn't a coincidence. I came here deliberately to see you again.'

'But why?'

Kerim chuckled. 'I like you when you pretend to be innocent. Surely this is not the first time you have been pursued by a man who finds you attractive. I would like to buy you a coffee, we could talk for a small time.'

'But I must get back to the convent?'

'Immediately? If your convent were ablaze with fire it would not be in such dire straits as my heart.'

She laughed, and then cocked her head

155

on one side. Her eyes were dark and sparkling as they looked into his own.

'Perhaps not immediately,' she relented. 'I can give you half an hour. Get into the car and we will go to a café for coffee.'

* * *

Kerim saw her on two further occasions during the week that followed, meeting her again for coffee when she made her twice-weekly shopping expeditions for the convent. Their friendship ripened over each stolen half hour and finally he dared to suggest that she should have dinner with him one evening. She protested, as he had expected that she would.

'But, Kerim, you know that I cannot. I am only allowed out of the convent to come shopping.'

'But why? You are not a nun, you do not wear a nun's robe!'

Dalia hesitated uncertainly. 'No, I am not a nun. I am — simply a servant at the convent. But they would not approve.'

'But you would like to come and have dinner with me? You have no personal moral or religious objections?'

'Of course not. I would love to come — '

'Then come.' He smiled earnestly. 'Romance is all the more sweeter when it is flavoured with the spice of daring. You could slip through the gates without being seen by the nuns, and I would be waiting to sweep you away on a night of enchantment. Is that not worth the risk of a stern word from the mother superior of your convent.'

She laughed. 'It is not as easy as all that. This is not a fairy story from the Arabian Nights!'

'Perhaps not, but we can pretend. You will be the rich and beautiful princess, escaping from the castle of your wicked father, and I shall be your poor but handsome lover waiting in the moonlight.'

Her laughter came as easily as before, and drew curious and envious glances from the other customers of the café where they sat over their coffee.

'Kerim, you are impossible.'

'Dalia, you are breaking my heart. You

must escape from your cruel castle and meet me this very night!'

They exchanged more smiles, and then she lowered her eyes. For a moment she was silent, and Kerim chose that moment to cover her hand with his own as it lay upon the table. She responded to his touch and looked up, and now his eyes were serious and hopeful. Dalia smiled again and turned her hand to clasp his own.

'All right, Kerim. I will try. It is not possible to get through the gate without being seen, but I think that I can get out through my bedroom window. But you must wait for me on the main road. Promise me that you will not come near the convent.'

'I promise.' He squeezed her hand gently. 'And tonight I shall be waiting.'

★ ★ ★

The moon shone benignly as he kept his promise later that evening, and he waited for almost an hour before he saw her slim figure hurrying down the road from the convent. He stepped away from the cypress tree that had shadowed him and she ran the last few yards into his arms. He kissed her lightly, and saw that even in the moonlight her face was flushed and excited. She said breathlessly:

'It was not as difficult as I thought. I had to pretend a headache so that I could retire early to my room, but no one saw me leave.'

Kerim smiled and put his arm around her waist as he led her to his car.

He had planned the evening carefully, avoiding any ostentatious night life but choosing a restaurant where they could wine and dine in comfort and good taste. The lights were shaded and he had specified a table where they might have some small measure of privacy. It was situated in old Jerusalem and Dalia smiled her approval as he led her inside.

Her tastes were simple and they ate charcoal grilled kebab with white rice and grilled tomatoes. The tiny pieces of skewered meat were spiced and flavoured, and Kerim ordered a bottle of dry Syrian wine to accompany the meal. At first Dalia declined to drink, but then gave way under gentle persuasion. She smiled and laughed frequently as she sipped her wine, or drew the pieces of kebab smoothly from the steel skewers with her even white teeth, and Kerim sensed that she was genuinely enjoying herself. He signalled a discreet waiter to bring another bottle of wine, and this time her protest was nothing but a formal joke that broke quickly into more laughter.

She asked him many more questions about himself and his work, and although Kerim answered frankly he was careful not to press her in return. Instead he devoted himself to flattering and teasing attentions, designed to make her relaxed and happy.

Only once did their conversation take a serious turn. An argument disturbed them from another table where a group of Arabs had become heated over the possibility of war with Israel. Dalia paused to listen, and then looked directly at Kerim.

'What will you do when the war comes?' she asked.

She had become abruptly sober, and Kerim noted that her tone had no doubts about the eventuality of war. Like Jackson she knew that it would happen. He replied just as soberly.

'If there is a war I shall return to the Lebanon to join the army. My country is certain to unite with the Arab cause.'

'Then you will help us to drive Israel into the sea?'

Her face had become fervent and he answered with a hard smile.

'When the war comes Israel is dead. They cannot stand against all the Arab armies. This time the Lebanon, Jordan, Egypt and Syria will all stand as one. Allah will be with us and we shall not fail.'

He paused and then touched her hand, smiling more gently.

'But this is not the night to talk of war. Tonight you are a princess, and I am your poor but handsome lover.'

Dalia laughed and relaxed, but seemed a little relieved to know where his sympathies lay. The evening continued and became more intimate over coffee and brandy.

Finally she had to remind him that it was getting late and he consented to drive her home. She sat close beside him as they left Jerusalem, and when he stopped the car by the side road turning leading to the convent she did not move away. Kerim turned to face her and she came willingly into his arms. Her lips answered slowly at first, but then their kiss was long and warm.

At last she drew back and said uncertainly:

'I must go now. Will you — will you walk with me a little way?'

Kerim became wary, a note of warning singing in his brain. He had known from the start that he could be ensnared in his own trap, and to leave the car and walk with her to the convent would be inviting it to spring. If Dalia had been well-trained she should have reported his interest in her to Rashid after their first encounter, and now the standard procedure would be for her to lead him to a suitable spot where the Egyptian and

162

a group of his more efficient students could lay in wait. His capture would be followed by savage interrogation.

The obvious dangers were balanced by the fact that if he did not accept her invitation then he would arouse suspicions that might not yet be there. During the evening he had formed the conclusion that she had been pleased to escape from the convent, and that the close life and hard training had made her ripe for rebellion. He felt that she had enjoyed herself too fully to have been deceiving him, but if he was wrong in his analysis then he was making another wrong decision now and might soon be dead.

He said calmly, 'Of course I'll walk with you, all the way if you like.'

She smiled. 'No, just a little way. Any further would not be safe.'

They got out of the car and Kerim put his arm around her as they walked slowly along the unmade road. The crickets twittered in the long yellow grass, and the moonlight threw long, black spear blade shadows from the tall cypresses

163

that bordered the road. Dalia was silent and content, but Kerim's mouth was a little dry.

They walked up into the hills and then descended into the dark lake of the lemon and orange groves. The grim outline of the convent was showing faint glimmers of light on the far side of the shallow valley, and Kerim could feel his heart beginning to beat more nervously as they entered the first of the lemon groves. Here there was cover for an ambush and if he had made the wrong decision it was too late. He was not even armed, for it was not easy to conceal a weapon from a woman in a close embrace and while accompanying Dalia he had deemed it best not to carry his automatic on his person.

Dalia's steps became slower and she stopped. Kerim halted beside her and felt his muscles tense as she looked into his face. He was alert for the first rustle of leaves and the rush of bodies, but none came.

She said simply, 'It is not safe for you to come any further, Kerim. I must say goodnight to you here.'

He smiled, and inside him the tension began to relax. Their faces came close and he kissed her for the second time, and then her arms were close around him. There was still no rush of attacking footsteps, and by mutual consent they moved off the road and into the dark, concealing shadows of the lemon grove. Dalia's kisses became fiercer and more abandoned, and she began moaning soft but fervent endearments of love.

Her arms were tight around him, and as they kissed her body seemed to weaken so that Kerim was fully supporting her weight. He lowered her gently towards the ground and her mouth became even more moist and yielding as her hands clung to his shoulders. She allowed him to lay her down on the soft grass, and then the strength seemed to flow back into her body as she pulled him closer. He lay beside her and felt the smooth, warm flesh of her thigh beneath his fingertips. Their mouths were still merging and blending together and now she was breathing fast and hard. Her body squirmed beneath him and then her hand fastened on his wrist, drawing his own hand closer beneath her dress and between her legs.

He knew then what she needed and it was not until after her last shuddering sigh that he began to feel the bitter stabs of his conscience. He remembered Schererzade, realizing that by now she must have arrived in Tel Aviv, and wondering whether she too had resorted to using her body for the age-old purposes of espionage. Then Dalia stirred him with a kiss, whispering that they must meet again, and his hatred for Jackson began to fester into solid loathing.

10

In the Lemon Grove

The following night Kerim again met Dalia in the lemon grove where they had made love; and it was the first of many such brief, stolen meetings by moon or starlight. She refused to repeat their first excursion and spend another whole evening with him in Jerusalem, saying that it was too dangerous for her to risk being seen, and also that she did not dare to leave the convent for more than an hour at a time. This new arrangement suited Kerim perfectly, even though he found it slightly ironic that he should now be holding these clandestine meetings so close to the very spot from which he had kept up his observations on the villa during the preceding weeks. These daytime watches he now dropped altogether in order to concentrate on his friendship with Dalia.

He was still sharply aware of the dangers surrounding him, but after that first uncertain occasion he made precautions for his safety. He always made a point of arriving early for their meetings, and then hiding his .38 automatic close to the roots of one of the lemon trees beside their favourite bower. The long grass covered the weapon completely, and the slide was drawn back with a round in position all ready to fire. Afterwards he would retrieve the gun when Dalia had returned to the convent.

The secret drama of their meetings seemed to provide Dalia with an excitement that increased her passion, and her love-making was always warm and eager. In between the quick spurts of her desires she would lay quietly in his arms in the near darkness beneath the lemon trees, content in the cool night beneath the starry glory of the sky. They would talk in low, murmuring voices, and Kerim sensed that what had started out for Dalia as a rebellious sexual adventure was slowly turning into something deeper and emotional. She was beginning to fall in love with him. Kerim's self-respect began to deteriorate, but he continued with his job.

He allowed her the lead in all their conversations, even though he was now certain that she had no suspicions at all. Mostly she was loving and gay, but when her thoughts did stray to politics and reality Kerim was in full agreement with her views. He championed the Arab cause and cursed the very existence of Israel. Dalia's confidence and affections for him increased, and after the third of their meetings she confessed to him the facts that he already knew. It came at the end of their hour together when he tempted her to stay in his arms a little longer. She said sadly:

'No, Kerim, you know that I would like to stay. But I must get back to my room before I am missed.'

He smiled. 'Are you so afraid of some elderly nuns who can only chastise you with stern words.'

She hesitated and then said, 'You do not understand, Kerim. I have not been

169

exactly truthful with you.' She hesitated for another long moment before meeting his eyes and then said, 'Kerim, I shall meet a much harsher fate than stern words if I am caught. That is why I must be so careful.'

Kerim raised himself on one elbow, and then said vaguely:

'But I don't understand.'

Dalia's reluctance lasted only another moment, and then she kissed him impulsively and explained.

'Kerim, the convent is not a school for young ladies any more. I have deceived you. It is now a training school for desert commandos who will strike the first blows in the war against Israel. I am not just an ordinary servant girl. I am being trained with others to take part in the coming battle. It is all very secret and no one must know, not even our own people. That is why I am not supposed to leave the convent, and why it will be so dangerous if I am caught.'

Kerim stared at her, and then laughed.

'This is another game, but our old game was better. You are not a desert commando, you are my princess.'

'But it is not a game. It is the truth.' She was eager to convince him now and rushed on. 'There are twelve students altogether, and two others are women like myself. We are all trained in sabotage, in how to handle firearms, in self-defence and in every form of espionage. Our instructor has come all the way from the United Arab Republic especially to teach us these skills. When the war comes we will be the first to attack Israel. We have all been given special targets which we are to destroy.'

She was so earnest that even if he had not known that she was telling the truth he would have believed her. He was silent for a moment, and then asked:

'But why do you tell me now?'

'Because I want to be honest with you, and because I know that you hate Israel just as much as we do. I have been thinking, Kerim, that perhaps you might join us. It would be wonderful for us to train and fight together. I could introduce you to Rashid, our instructor, and I am sure that he would accept you as a recruit.'

Kedim felt a sudden flicker of alarm in his stomach, and realized that things had gone almost too far and that she had learned to trust him too implicitly. He was standing on a very slippery slope indeed and if she did mention him to Rashid in the hope of having him enlisted into the spy school then both of them would very soon be dead. The Egyptian would never be fooled in the same way that Dalia had been.

He pretended to think her suggestion over, and then shook his head as though reluctantly.

'It would be wonderful, Dalia, but it is not possible. When the war comes I shall have to return to the Lebanon. I am already a reserve officer in the army so my duty is plain.' He saw the disappointment in her face, and then went on more quietly, 'But in any case, how would you explain me to this man Rashid? You will have to admit that you have been leaving the convent without his permission to meet me, and he will be very angry that you have disobeyed his orders. You have already told me that your treatment will be harsh if you are caught.'

Dalia nodded slowly, and he saw that his last point was one that she had not calculated. He kissed her before she could find an argument and said:

'I am pleased that you too are actively engaged in the Arab struggle against Israel, but when the time comes we must each do our duty in different ways.' He paused then, weighing his next move before saying doubtfully, 'But now that you have told me of this I am not sure that we should continue to see each other in this way. I did not realize what terrible risks you have been taking.'

'But we must see each other again.' Her voice became anxious and she went on earnestly, 'The risks are not so great. They have trained me to get in and out of such places unseen, and I am very careful. Please, Kerim, do not worry for me.'

She was close in his arms and he lay back and allowed her to kiss him, slowly

173

tightening their embrace. Her body was warm and gently moving on top of him, and when she lifted her head her dark hair hung forward like a soft curtain to screen both their faces. She said fretfully:

'Please, Kerim, say that you will continue to see me.'

He smiled and made an affirmative nod of his head. Then their embrace tightened and he knew that he had to make love to her again before they parted.

★ ★ ★

Their fleeting liaison continued through the nights that followed, and in between their loving and kisses Kerim gradually built up a more complete picture of what was happening inside the convent. The Jordanian students were all being thoroughly trained to commit acts of terrorism towards Israel, again with special attention being paid to their tuition in handling weapons and plastic explosives. At present their instruction was limited to the classroom level, either because Rashid did not consider them sufficiently advanced for more practical training, or because he had been unable to find a similar training ground to the convenient disused quarry in Syria.

It was all exactly as Kerim had expected, and it was somewhat frustrating to find that even now he could not progress much farther. Dalia had told him that the Jordanian students all had specific targets to destroy inside Israeli Jerusalem and deeper inside Israel, but he soon realized that she did not know what these specific targets were. They would be named only when the time came for the blows to be struck. However, she was convinced that there was not much time left, for their training programme was being rushed through as fast as possible.

Kerim realized that he would learn nothing more in this direction, and so he concentrated on trying to build up a more definite picture of Rashid. Again he was mostly frustrated, he already knew that Rashid was Egyptian and had been sent from Cairo, and only one more positive fact emerged. Rashid was the star pupil of a long established and very efficient espionage training school near Cairo; a school that was run for the Egyptian secret service by a wanted German war criminal who had escaped from Europe at the close of the second world war. The rest of Rashid's personal background was unknown.

Kerim dared not appear to be too inquisitive, and could only ask occasional questions and hope that Dalia would develop them herself. One night he asked whether Rashid had any interests outside the convent, and the answer was negative. Only once had Dalia known him to go outside the convent since his arrival there, and then he had gone simply to tour the holy sites of Jerusalem. It was then that she remarked that Rashid was interested in religion, for he had photographs and detailed drawings of the most important churches in a drawer in his desk. The statement was out of character with the man and gave Kerim food for puzzled thought, but finally he dismissed it. No villain was ever wholly black, just as no hero could be purely white, so there was no reason why the Egyptian should not have a private interest in either religious history or theology.

* * *

It soon became obvious that their dangerous affair could not last indefinitely, despite Dalia's confidence that Rashid had trained her well enough to evade his vigilance night after night. The convent was large enough for each student to be allotted a separate room, and she had made a habit of leaving and re-entering through her window at the back of the convent with the aid of a thin nylon rope. However, Kerim knew that it could only be a matter of time before someone found her room empty during her absence, or else noticed her hurrying figure in the starlight as she ran down the hillside to enter the lemon groves, and then disaster would swiftly descend upon them both. Their time was running out, and once he was satisfied that he had learned all that she knew he faced the problem of how to disengage before her nocturnal jaunts were discovered.

It was a difficult task, for Dalia had become possessive and her answer to their danger was to renew her suggestion that Kerim should be introduced into the fold of spies. She refused to accept a parting and insisted on discussing various ways and means by which he might become a member of the spy school without Rashid learning of their midnight dalliances in the lemon grove.

Kerim was in a quandry, for he knew that any such move would be suicide on his part and probably for Dalia also, yet at the same time he could not break off their relationship without some acceptable understanding. He understood the hell-like fury of a woman scorned, and feared that if he did stop seeing her she might reveal the true facts to Rashid, which would put the Egyptian on his guard, and again would probably cost her her life. Kerim simply could not see how he could guarantee her safety from the dangers of her own emotions once he withdrew.

The problem caused him to continue their clandestine meetings until it was too late, and he was to curse himself bitterly for ever afterwards, blaming his own indecision for what eventually took place.

On their last night together she appeared as usual an hour before midnight. He heard the rustling of leaves as she came through the lemon grove and then she hurried into his arms. They kissed and her lips were warm and eager as always, and then she threw back her head and smiled at him, her dark eyes reflecting a sparkle of starlight.

'Kerim,' she said excitedly. 'It is to be soon. The war with Israel! Rashid has told us today that we must work harder. There is not much more time to prepare.'

'Did he say how long?'

'No, only that there is not much more time, but it is to be soon. Oh, Kerim, I shall be so glad when the war does come. It will mean that we must part and that you will have to return to your unit in the Lebanon. You will be called into active service. But then we shall destroy Israel. Destroy them completely and then there will be peace. When it is over you and I will meet again. Then we — '

She became abruptly silent, her body becoming stiff and rigid in his arms. Kerim had heard the faint movement of the leaves behind them in the same instant and twisted quickly away. He was trapped in her embrace and he was an age too late. The lemon trees rustled more loudly and the black silhouette of a man emerged from the darkness.

Dalia released her breath in a sharp gasp of alarm, and then there was a moment of frigid silence. The dark shadow came closer from the gloom, and his teeth flashed briefly in a tight, slightly twisted smile. Kerim had already seen the dark glint of the large black automatic in his hand, and his stomach fluttered more violently as he recognized the make. It was a heavy Russian Stechkin APS, fitted with a twenty shot magazine and capable of being fired fully automatic like a handsized machine gun.

Mahmoud Abdel Rashid said calmly:

'Dalia, you are a very stupid young woman. Just lately you have had too many headaches, and have retired too early too often to your room. Explain now! Who is this man?'

Dalia panicked. The combined menace of Rashid's stance and tone seemed to shatter her nerve and trigger an impulse reaction. Afterwards Kerim could never decide whether she had been abruptly afraid for herself, or whether she had deliberately sacrificed herself in the hope of giving him a chance to live. Whatever her reason some blind instinct had revealed to her that they could expect no mercy from the Egyptian. She thrust with both hands at Kerim's chest, pushing him away and crying out to him to run. And then she twisted round and attempted to flee for her life through the darkened lemon grove.

Kerim had overbalanced and fallen to one knee, and Rashid temporarily ignored him, following the animal law of nature to chase the prey that took flight. The

181

Egyptian turned his body smoothly, his arm outstretched in the classic text-book pose, the big Russian automatic aimed at eye level. If he had fired fully automatic the gun would have arced a wide spray of bullets and probably missed, but Rashid fired three fast single shots. The three explosions sounded almost as one and Dalia screamed as they blasted her running figure forwards off her feet, sprawling her face down amongst the lemon trees.

Kerim had thrown himself sideways, reaching desperately for his own .38 automatic that lay hidden in the grass only a few yards away. He was blessed by the only thing that could have saved him, and that was the pure luck of finding the automatic first time. Rashid was swivelling to face him, fast bringing the big 9mm Stechkin to bear on its second target, and Kerim rolled in another scrambling move of desperation as he fired the .38. Rashid's head jerked up and he made a gagging cry as the bullet struck into his throat, and then a last shot from the Stechkin clipped a shower of leaves from the branch beside Kerim's head as the Egyptian crumpled up and fell. Kerim was sweating hard and there was a threat of nausea in the pit of his stomach.

Slowly Kerim struggled to his feet. Rashid lay still and very dead, and after a moment Kerim turned away through the lemon grove to the spot where Dalia had fallen. She was still alive when he knelt beside her and gently turned her over, but her eyes were hurt and filled with pain and she could not speak. He could feel her blood spreading through his fingers where he tried to support her back, but there was nothing that he could do. He stared into her face, and after half a minute he slowly realized that there was no more life in her glazed eyes.

He lowered her then to the ground, and with his fingers gently closed her eyelids. When he removed his hand the lids slowly opened again. For the second time he closed them, and for the second time they slowly opened to reveal her dead, accusing stare.

Horror stirred at the nausea inside him,

and then he became aware of noise and lights radiating from the direction of the convent. The sound of the shooting had carried clearly in the night and he had to leave.

He rose to his feet and hurried away, but behind him Dalia's open eyes still gazed up at the stars, and his right hand was still thickly stained with her blood.

11

Plague of Evils

Jackson was furious.

Kerim had not risked making a midnight telephone call which might have aroused suspicion if any kind of a check was made, and had delayed contacting the Amman number until nine a.m. the following morning when Mazhar Air Freight & Exports would ostensibly be open for business. He had asked for Mister Aziz Mazhar, and as usual had been told to call back later. He had then hinted bluntly that the matter was serious before ringing off, and the Major and Williamson had appeared in Jerusalem within a matter of hours.

It was Williamson who made the contact. The young Englishman came boldly into the Petra Hotel, propped himself against the bar, complained loudly about the heat, and drank a bottle

185

of beer. Kerim saw him and left the hotel without making any acknowledgement. Ten minutes later Williamson came out and headed directly into the descending, stepped street that ran into the bazaars. Kerim followed him through the maze of stone archways, along a zig-zag route that circled past the Holy Sepulchre towards the Damascus gate. When they emerged from the bazaar streets Kerim closed with the man ahead.

Williamson said calmly:

'Nice morning, isn't it. The Major is waiting in the car. If things are going wrong then it won't be safe to sit in a café. Too much risk of being overheard.'

Kerim nodded in agreement but made no comment. They climbed up wide, ascending steps lined with small shops to pass through the great, arched exit of the Damascus gate. Outside the brown medieval walls Kerim recognized the black American sedan that Williamson had been driving in Amman and they went directly to it. Williamson took the wheel while Kerim climbed in beside him. Jackson was sitting patiently in the back.

A polite, smartly uniformed young member of the Jordanian Tourist Police saluted and waved them on as Williamson started the car and turned right towards the Jericho Road. If he had attempted to go left towards forbidden Israel the policeman would have tactfully stopped him.

Williamson drove slowly and Kerim turned in his seat to face his employer. He had not slept the previous night after his return from the convent and he knew that it showed. Jackson had leaned forward and his face was bleak and demanding.

'Well, what's the trouble?'

Kerim told him. Jackson listened in silence but his face gradually became more savage. Then he exploded.

'You mean that you've killed Rashid? You bloody fool, that was the last thing we wanted. Why the devil didn't you break away from this girl before it was too late? Surely you must have realized that she couldn't carry on fooling a man like Rashid? It must have been obvious that eventually he would follow her and

187

catch the two of you playing hanky panky in the bushes? Or is that why you stayed? Did you get so damned fond of screwing her that you didn't want to break it off?'

Kerim stiffened, but the back of the car seat was a barrier between them. He controlled the physical surge of his anger and said coldly:

'For that I could be tempted to kill you also. You and Rashid are two of a stinking kind.'

There was a moment of silence. Their eyes glared in a clash of blue and steel-grey menace, and then Jackson retreated. He said flatly:

'All right, I'll apologize for that last remark. There's no point in either of us getting temperamental. The fact remains that I didn't want Rashid dead, what I wanted was the facts of what he was planning. And you've literally screwed-up our chances of getting any closer to that.'

They had left Jerusalem and there was less traffic to distract Williamson's attention. The younger man sensed the

188

need for a peace-maker to break up the hostile atmosphere in the car and diverted them by asking:

'What happens next? Will the spy school disperse, or is it possible that the convent will be used as before under a new instructor?'

Jackson tugged dubiously at his jaw and gave the question some thought.

'I don't know, Bill. The usual form would be to disperse the students as fast as possible, and then have them lay low until a replacement for Rashid could be despatched from Cairo. Then they would have to regroup elsewhere. But we can't treat this as normal, events are hotting up and we know that they haven't got much more time to finish their training. Unless they already have alternative premises that they can move into without any loss of time, then it's possible that they'll risk continuing with the convent. Remember that Rashid has certainly been working with Jordanian approval, despite his preference for keeping things quiet. If he's managed to impart even basic security to his students then they will have removed both bodies from that lemon grove sometime during last night, including all the ejected cartridge shells. Everything will be tidy and nothing will be reported, at least not to the police. And if the police do get wind of it from the outside there'll almost certainly be a swift word from above to tell them to drop the matter. This spy school is no crime against Jordan, it's kept hush-hush simply because they don't want it advertised.'

He continued to rub at his jaw, and then went on:

'After last night they obviously know that there has been a leak, although they probably think that it was an Israeli agent who was prowling around. But even so they can carry on using the convent as soon as a new instructor arrives, only now they will tighten their security. They'll double their guards, keep a sharper lookout, and the next prowler will be practically dead on sight. I can't risk sending Kerim, or any other agent in to continue observation, so from our point of view it doesn't matter whether they shift their base or not, we're completely blocked from getting any farther forward.'

Kerim said slowly, 'What about the Syrian school near Damascus. They don't know that they're compromised, and the villa is better situated for a continuous watch. Barek may tighten his security when he learns what has happened to Rashid here in Jerusalem, but he has no real reason to suppose that his own school is in any danger.'

Jackson nodded. His initial fury had cooled but he was still angry. He said tartly:

'I had thought of that. We'll have to stay clear of the convent altogether, and Barek is our only practical lead. But I'm not sending you back to Damascus. Some smart airport or border official might notice that you're making a habit of popping backwards and forwards, and then they'll wonder why. There are too many stamps on your passport, and if you arouse suspicion and get nailed then they might tumble to the fact that we do know about Barek's outfit. Then this mess will be complete. I don't intend to take that risk so I'll find another agent to cover the Damascus end. You will fade out of the picture.'

Kerim's mouth curled in a half smile.

'That will suit me fine. I am already sick to death of this whole business.'

Jackson gave him a hard look, but then relaxed.

'All right, I suppose you have earned a break. And perhaps it's not wholly your fault that things have gone wrong. Life seems to be a plague of evils at the moment. You'd better fill me in on anything new you learned from the girl before she and Rashid were killed.'

'There wasn't much. She did tell me some things about Rashid himself, but that's hardly helpful now. He was trained at a special espionage school in Cairo, and she mentioned something about a German spymaster who was in charge.'

Jackson frowned. 'We do know a little about that. Nasser employs quite a few Nazis, although he tries to keep the actual war criminals out of sight. The man she mentioned is most probably a certain Otto Wolffe who was one of the top men of the SD, the intelligence and security service set up within Heydrich's SS. We've had reports that Wolffe has been responsible for training quite a lot of Nasser's agents, and it's also rumoured that the Israelies have made a couple of suicide efforts to get him out of Egypt. They've lost several good men. Wolffe had a pathological hatred for the Jews even before Hitler decided upon his final solution to the Jewish problem, that's why he fled to Cairo after the war where he has a common bond with his hosts. Now the Shinbeth would dearly love to get their hands on him, he's one of their top targets.'

Kerim said bitterly, 'You seem to know more than I do. Dalia died for nothing.'

'The girl died because she was careless. If she had lived to carry out the job she was being trained for she would probably have been shot dead crossing the frontier with Israel, so don't let it bother you. Was there anything else you can tell me?'

Kerim was silent for a moment, controlling his tongue, and then slowly he detailed all the little scraps of information that he had built up from their conversations together. While he talked he had to concentrate on keeping Dalia's dead, accusing stare out of his mind.

Jackson did not interrupt or ask any questions, but allowed him to tell the story his own way and in his own time. Williamson still concentrated on his driving as the big car cruised steadily along the Jericho road. When the report was finished there was another brief silence, and it was Kerim himself who broke it.

'A little while ago you mentioned that events were hotting up, and then something about a plague of evils, what else has gone wrong?'

Jackson said shortly, 'Haven't you read the papers, or listened to a radio within the past few hours?'

'No, I have not.' Kerim faced the blue eyes of his employer and again his temper was shortening. 'Neither have I slept, and neither have I eaten. It has not been a normal morning.'

Jackson laughed rather sourly. 'I'll agree with that. For your information, and to quote the newspaper headlines, the Middle East situation is now at flashpoint. Nasser has ordered the United Nations Peace Keeping Force to pull out of the Sinai. If that happens then there is nothing at all to stop the balloon going up. Egypt and Syria have alerted all their armed forces and are moving their troops towards Israel. It's now a matter of days, depending on how long the UN can hold out before they are forced to withdraw.'

Some faint intuition made Kerim sense that there was more.

'Is that all?'

'It's enough,' Jackson retorted. 'But just to complete my morning I've also heard that your little friend Schererzade has been arrested in Israel. She arrived in Tel Aviv only five days ago, and already the Shinbeth have picked her up as a British spy.'

'Schererzade!' Kerim spoke sharply and the rest of it had abruptly dwindled in importance. 'But how? What exactly has happened?'

'I'm damned if I know. Something went wrong. The man who was arranging her job in the night club was caught with her. I think he was the one who was spotted.'

'But what will happen to Schererzade?'

'Jail if she's lucky. Otherwise they might shoot her. I have a feeling that in this part of the world it isn't going to be a very good year for spies, the ones that get caught that is.'

'But you could get her out?'

Jackson shook his head. 'Not this time. The Shinbeth make much tougher opposition than the Egyptians, and there's a big difference between an open hospital in peace-time Cairo and a maximum security jail in Tel Aviv where the whole population is alert and mobilized for war. This time there is nothing that I can do and she'll have to take her chances. I can't send you or anybody else to get her out.'

Kerim controlled his struggling emotions and kept his mouth shut. Jackson had clearly made up his mind upon the subject and professionally he was right. Any argument would be futile and a waste of words. Jackson waited for a moment but when nothing was said he turned to Williamson.

'This is far enough, Bill. I don't think that there is anything more to discuss. We'll take Kerim back to Jerusalem and then return to Amman.'

'Right, Major.'

Williamson braked the car and pulled to a stop.

Kerim said slowly, 'And what am I expected to do now? Do you want me to lay off for a couple of days and then check out whether the convent is still being used as a spy school?'

'No, it's not safe. Stay away from the convent altogether. In fact, get right out of Jerusalem. A too hasty departure might arouse suspicion so you'd best spend a couple of days working on your cover. Take some more pictures for magazines. Then get a plane back to Beirut and take a holiday until I contact you again.'

Kerim nodded his understanding, for

he was still having difficulty in concealing his inner feelings. The car was now speeding swiftly on its return journey and Jackson began brooding with his own troubles. Williamson whistled a single bar of an absent-minded tune, and then realized what he was doing and concentrated earnestly on his driving. Apart from that the trip back into Jerusalem was wholly silent.

12

Into the Lion's Den

After the two Englishmen had left for Amman Kerim walked slowly back through the bazaars to the Petra Hotel. He barely noticed the lively bustle of movement around him, even when his shoulder was bumped repeatedly by passing bodies. He came out of the narrow, stepped street before the hotel and went into the bar. His throat was dry and his stomach was empty, and almost mechanically he asked for a beer. He drank it in slow-motion, barely noticing the taste, and then on sudden impulse he asked for a bottle of brandy.

He carried the bottle up to his room. The air was close and stuffy despite the open window and he stripped off his jacket and shirt, throwing them untidily across a chair. He stared at the bottle for a moment, his face hard and unblinking, and then with deliberate fingers he broke the seal. He half filled a tooth glass, and then brought it up to the three-quarter level with water from the wash basin tap. Carefully he placed the bottle and the glass on the small table beside his bed. He lay down on top of the bed and stared without seeing at the dull white ceiling. It was a long time before he reached out his hand for the glass, but then he drank steadily and he drank all day.

He was making a mistake. He was ignoring Jackson's sound advice to go out and protect his cover, but Jackson and his cover were no longer important. Instead he thought of Schererzade.

Schererzade.

Her face pale and helpless, her eyes closed and her hair spread like a dark halo on the white hospital pillows. Schererzade with her face in pain, and then slowly with returning life and laughter. Schererzade in his arms as he lifted her still crippled body from his car on to the grassy hillside during those final sunny days on Cyprus. Schererzade smiling with the glow of health coming back into her sun-darkened cheeks. Schererzade with her lips trembling close against his own during their one and only kiss. Schererzade laughing, smiling, kissing, screaming — for Schererzade was now in the hands of the Shinbeth, the coldly efficient and unemotional Israeli Intelligence Service.

Schererzade dead.

And then Dalia.

Dalia with her eyes that would not close. Dalia with her dead, accusing stare gazing up at the stars. Serious, loving, passionate Dalia. Dalia with her hungry mouth and the eager, demanding body he had come to know so well. Dalia with her arms and legs locked tightly around him in the lemon grove, moaning, pleading. Dalia with three 9mm bullets in her back. Dalia who had died for nothing.

Schererzade.

Schererzade's face with Dalia's eyes. Schererzade's eyes with Dalia's dying agony. Eyes that would not close. Eyes that stared for ever. And blood smothering his hand. Dalia's blood. Schererzade's blood. Dalia dead. Schererzade dead. Schererzade's face with Dalia's eyes.

Kerim reached for the glass and it was empty. His fingers fumbled for the bottle and that was empty too. He was sweating feverishly in the stifling heat and the sheets beneath him were wet and plastered to his naked back. He stared at the empty bottle and then made the long, weary effort to sit up.

His mind cleared a little, and after a moment he got unsteadily to his feet. He stripped naked and stumbled to the shower, switching on the cold jet and shuddering under its impact. He stayed there for ten minutes and then came out feeling partially sobered but very sick in the stomach. He dried and dressed, and then hesitated before leaving his room. He was on the top floor and he climbed slowly up the last flight of stairs to emerge on the flat roof.

It was late in the afternoon, but the sun was still powerful enough to make him screw up his eyes. It was several moments before he could open them and keep them open, and then he walked across the roof to gaze out over old Jerusalem. The great sixteenth-century walls built by Suleiman the Magnificent ringed the city in a tight circle. The ancient brown and grey stone of its churches and buildings lay warm and mellowed in the sun, while the great golden Dome Of The Rock gleamed like a colossal yellow pearl. Beyond the city lay the quiet olive groves of the garden of Gethsemane, and above them the tiny, onion-spired Russian church of St. Mary Magdalene built on the slope of the Mount of Olives. The scene was peaceful, and flavoured with the memories of its past.

Kerim stood for a moment, and then turned away and walked back across the flat roof. Behind the hotel was a small clear space filled with parked cars, including his own hired Fiat, and then the great rampart of David's Tower and the city wall. Beyond the wall the Israeli half of divided Jerusalem looked just as hot, dusty and deceptively peaceful. Somewhere in the threatened land behind that wall was Schererzade.

Dalia intruded into his thoughts again, for they were still inextricably mixed. During the past few hours he had become certain that Dalia had begun to suspect that he was a spy. His refusal to declare themselves to Rashid and join her openly at the convent had caused her to suspect him subconsciously, even though she had not been willing to admit the fact to herself. When Rashid had surprised them together she had known instinctively that he was a doomed man, and love had caused her to throw away her own life to give him his chance to survive. That was the way he saw things now. It explained what he had first mistaken for blind panic. And it meant that he had killed her.

Dalia was dead.

And Schererzade was a prisoner beyond the wall.

Schererzade was a captured spy, and this was going to be a bad year for captured spies. Both Arabs and Jews were all set, they were on their marks and all ready for the word go. Only the starting signal was needed for war, and in war-time spies were shot. There was no time for trials, only firing squads.

Schererzade's face with Dalia's eyes.

For a very long time Kerim stared out over the wall, and then at last he descended into the hotel once more. It was not precisely a matter of making a decision, but more a gradual and growing realization that the decision was made. He went down to the bar and purchased a second bottle of brandy, and then he returned to his room.

He poured a stiff drink but left it untouched. He stood the glass upon the small dressing table and sat down in the chair before it. His hand fumbled as he found a paper and pen, but steadied again as he began to write.

He wrote a brief letter of resignation to Jackson with no explanations, and carefully signed his name. Next he addressed an envelope to Mister Aziz Mazhar, care of Air Freight & Exports in Amman, and sealed the letter inside. Then he drank the brandy in a bitter, ironic toast, to the past, the present, and if there was to be any, to the future.

★ ★ ★

He awoke the next morning with a thunderous headache, feeling weak and deathly and with a dry, searing taste in his mouth. It required an almost herculean effort to raise his head from the pillow, and he felt only a little better when he had showered and shaved. He forced himself to drink several cups of black coffee, and then ventured out into the streets to post his resignation to Jackson.

On his return he drank more black coffee and forced himself to eat some lightly buttered bread rolls. It was a minimum breakfast but at least it helped to settle his stomach. Afterwards he returned to his room to pack his few belongings, and then he settled his account and left the hotel. He drove the small Fiat back to the garage from which he had hired it and settled his account there, and then picked up his suitcase and walked slowly but steadily towards the Mandelbaum gate, the only crossing point between Jordan and Israel, and one from which there was no return. The crossing could only be made one way.

The Mandelbaum Gate was not exactly a gate at all, despite its impressive name. Instead it was just a ruined house in an area of ruined houses, with a road block and armed sentries. The sun was hot and Kerim's head was swimming as he approached, and although he could not see them he was aware of armed troops watching vigilantly from high vantage points. He could sense the hostile eyes, and wondered how many rifles might be lined up casually, or even hopefully, upon his chest.

Cold-faced Jordanian control officials inspected him and his passport. A curt order made him open his suitcase and arrogant hands turned over his contents. His two cameras were examined, and his status as a journalist closely questioned. Kerim could sense the enmity of these men, and the violent hatred for anyone even remotely friendly to Israel. He began to sweat and could feel his heart pounding. Then his passport was stamped and he was reminded that he could not return.

He was through, into the lion's den. He walked to the Israeli checkpoint, presented his passport and waited for the inevitable question.

'Where is your visa, your entry permit?'

Kerim said quietly. 'I didn't have time to get one. My name is Kerim Soiron and I am an agent of the British Military Intelligence department for the Middle East. I have some information which I think will be useful to your own Intelligence service and I wish to defect to Israel.'

13

A Hard Bargain

There were the inevitable hours of delay; questions, agitated conversations only just out of his hearing, more questions, frowns, hesitations and lengthy telephone calls. More questions, more confusion, more telephone calls and still more questions. Kerim refused to elaborate on his first statement until he had been taken under escort to the safer surroundings of a police station deeper inside Israeli Jerusalem. Here he faced an even tougher interrogation from a high ranking police officer, but again he refused to add more than the bare facts. At the border post he had simply asked to be conducted to a higher authority, but now he demanded that he be allowed to deal directly with a representative of the Shinbeth.

This far the Israelies had made no

definite decision on how to treat him, they were neither hostile nor friendly. He had been searched at the border post and had handed over his automatic, which had been viewed with suspicion. His interrogators were wary of a Jordanian plot and were admitting and accepting nothing, they plied their questions with a cautious reserve, and for long periods he was left alone with a single uncommunicative guard. In one respect he was glad of their suspicions and delays, he asked for and received endless cups of black coffee and was gradually shedding the worst effects of his hangover. Finally his captors began to lose patience and he had to give them the simple explanation.

'A few days ago your Shinbeth arrested a minor British spy in Tel Aviv. Now I am here to arrange a deal — my information for her release. And I will talk only to the Shinbeth.'

He was adamant against their insistence that he should be more explicit, resisting the increasing pressure of their questions and the first hints of threatened violence. For an hour he sat upright in a hard chair, harassed by the Police Chief and two determined Lieutenants, and then he was taken away and locked into a cell.

He guessed that the telephone wires would be humming again between Jerusalem and Tel Aviv, and took the opportunity to call a jailer to his cell door and request a meal. The man replied briefly that he would inform his officer, but there was a long delay and Kerim began to believe that the request had been denied. It was no more than he should have expected, for a hungry man is weakened and the weak talk more readily. He lay down on the single bunk and tried to relax, and then he was surprised by the jailer bringing him a tray of food.

There was a plate of vegetable and mutton stew and a flat pancake of unleavened bread. It was a meal to fill rather than to flatter him, which meant that they were still uncommitted. He was not yet regarded as a potential friend or a potential enemy. He smiled wryly and for a moment everything else became unimportant. This was the first meal he had faced since Dalia had died in the lemon grove and now he ate ravenously.

They came for him after another two hours, but he was not returned to the interrogation room. Instead he was taken outside under armed escort to a waiting car. He asked no questions and was told nothing as they bundled him into the back seat. One of the Police Lieutenants climbed in beside him, the other took the front seat beside the driver. The car drove off into the night and the road signs that appeared fleetingly in the sweeping beam of the headlights left no doubt that they were heading for Tel Aviv.

It was a fast, silent drive, taking a little less than an hour to cross the narrow waist of Israel to the principal new city on the Mediterranean coast. He saw little of Tel Aviv as the car sped through the darkened streets, for it was now past midnight and there was very little traffic. The car stopped before the bleak concrete façade of a police station and Kerim was ordered out and hurried quickly up the steps. The two Lieutenants flanked him on either side and his arrival was obviously expected. There were no questions or explanations and he was hustled past the reception desk, through a door and up a flight of stairs to the upper level of the building. Briskly he was propelled along a short corridor and then through another door into a bare, spartan room with only a table and two chairs. It was empty and here they stopped. The two policemen exchanged words in Hebrew and then looked at Kerim. One of them gestured to a chair.

'Sit down,' he ordered in Arabic. 'You will wait here. Do you understand?'

Kerim nodded, and slowly he sat down.

The two policemen went out and closed the door behind them. He was left alone.

★ ★ ★

Twenty minutes passed. There was silence. The room was soundproof and nothing penetrated from the corridor outside. Inside there was not even the

213

ticking of a clock. Kerim waited, sitting quietly in his chair and moving his eyes only once to examine the room. There was nothing to examine, just the empty desk in front of him, a second chair behind it, and a second door in the wall. The light was a single naked bulb hanging from the ceiling above his head. The waiting time was to wear at his nerves but he accepted it calmly, although he did not think that he was being observed. Finally the door behind the desk was opened and a man came into the room.

The man was tall and thin, dressed in a dark suit with a black tie. A black caricature of a man who would have blended perfectly into the background of a funeral. His face was long, narrowing at the jaw, and possessed all the warmth of hard grey concrete. He wore plain, square-lensed spectacles, and his smile of greeting was no more than a faint relaxation of his mouth. He said quietly:

'I am sorry that you have waited for so long. My arrival here was unavoidably delayed. My name is Reinhard.'

The words were in slightly guttural English. Kerim did not answer as he tried to weigh up his new opponent. Reinhard sat down behind the desk, rested his arms on the bare surface and continued as though there had been no pause.

'And your name is Kerim Soiron. French father, Egyptian mother. Raised and educated in Cairo. Worked for the American Central Intelligence Agency, and then for British Military Intelligence. Our dossier on you is thin, but it contains the basic facts. Now you wish to defect to the Israeli Intelligence Service. Why?'

'Are you an agent of the Shinbeth?'

Reinhard answered with another charade of a smile.

'Be assured, my friend. I am as close to the Shinbeth as you are likely to get. So far you have bluffed and refused to answer questions, wasting the valuable time of our police officers at the Mandelbaum Gate and again in Jerusalem. But now you can go no higher. If you wish to talk you will talk to me or not at all. I believe you once mentioned some kind of a deal?'

Kerim drew a breath and nodded, for instinct told him that he was at last dealing with the man he wanted. He said bluntly:

'A few days ago, here in Tel Aviv, your people arrested a young Arab girl named Schererzade. She came from Cyprus, sent into Israel as an agent for British Intelligence. Her job was only a minor one, simply to take up work in a suitable night club and pass on reports of current rumours and gossip. She was picked up soon after she arrived. That young woman was a close friend of mine. I want to help her, and I'm prepared to buy her release.'

Reinhard nodded. 'I know the woman. We suspected her when she applied for permission to come to Israel. She was one of our agents in Egypt but she returned to working for the British. We might have left her alone had conditions been normal, but Israel is now facing a war for survival and a purge has been necessary. During peace spies are a nuisance, but in times of war they become a danger, regardless of their politics or colour.

Schererzade was foolish and she paid the predictable price. Now she is being held in a maximum security jail.'

'What will happen to her?'

'At the moment she is awaiting trial. What happens will depend upon the temper of her judges. Perhaps a prison sentence, or perhaps she will be shot. Israel is now mobilizing for war. Perhaps you are not fully aware of our present situation. The United Nations have capitulated to Nasser's demands and are withdrawing their peace-keeping force. Egypt's army has been moved into the Sinai and there are now some fifty-eight thousand Egyptian troops poised along our southern frontier. Damascus radio claims that Syrian armed forces are at 'maximum preparedness' with a further twelve thousand troops massed on the north-east. Jordan's army has been put on alert and every Arab state from Iraq to Morocco has pledged its support for a holy war to massacre every Jew in Israel. You and your friend Schererzade may be playing children's games, Mr Soiron, but Israel is not.'

Reinhard paused to let his words sink in, and then asked coldly, 'What is the information that you have come to trade?'

'What guarantee have I that it will secure Schererzade's release?'

'You have none. But I will be frank with you. The girl is irrelevant. Israel faces a fight for her very survival, and the results will not be affected by whether your friend lives, dies, or rots in jail. If you have something that can help us then I will give you the girl.'

Kerim hesitated, and then slowly he nodded. Reinhard's eyes were blank pebbles behind his glasses and his face was completely lacking in any emotion, but Kerim knew that it was the fairest offer he would get. He said grimly:

'I can give you details of two special training schools set up by Egypt to turn young Syrians and Jordanians into agent-saboteurs for use against Israel. Each school is a limited community of twelve picked students, and each one will be given set targets to destroy. One school has been set up in Syria and the other in Jordan.'

Reinhard leaned back in his chair and laughed.

'And the training school in Syria is a large villa close to Damascus. It is at present being run by an Egyptian who calls himself Ahmed Barek. And you spent many long, weary weeks watching his activities from the nearest hillside.'

Kerim was staring hard and Reinhard explained.

'Your friend George who lives in Darrasa Street in Damascus is rather greedy. He accepts Israeli money as well as British. From George we know everything about this Syrian spy school. I even have copies of the photographs you took of its members. George's friend, whose darkroom you used to develop them, took an extra set of prints from the negatives.'

Kerim said savagely, 'I never did trust that blasted little pouf.'

Reinhard almost smiled. 'Don't worry about George. Your Syrian friend is predictable and he only has one more step to make. He already accepts pay from the British, and he already accepts pay from us. Next he will try to contact the Syrian Intelligence Service in the hope that he can extract payments from them also. Then either your Major Jackson or I will give the order, and George will have an unfortunate accident.'

Kerim had recovered his composure.

'There is still the spy school in Jordan. George could not have given you that location.'

'True, but when you left Damascus to follow Mahmoud Abdel Rashid into Jordan we guessed that you were on to a similar trail. What is the exact location?'

Kerim's hesitation was only fractional, he knew he could not play games with this man.

'They are using a convent school on the north road out of Jerusalem. It was originally the St Magdalene Convent school for young ladies. At the moment they're probably a bit disorganized. I killed Rashid two nights ago, and one of his girl students also died in the same gun battle.'

'Very careless of you,' was Reinhard's comment. 'But perhaps a favour to us. With Rashid dead there is hardly any time for anyone else to adequately replace him. This nest of Jordanian spies is no longer an immediate threat, and Ahmed Barek and his Syrians are being watched. Have you any idea what their precise targets were to be?'

Kerim shook his head. 'The students themselves have not been told.'

'It does not matter. For the whole of Israel's existence our frontiers have been plagued by Arab infiltration, terrorism, sabotage, murder raids and guerrilla warfare, and we have had much practice in dealing with such incidents. Of late our attackers have been receiving more and more specialized training, but still we find that we can handle them. No doubt these select schools organized by Rashid and Barek will be better trained and equipped than most, but their chances of survival are just as thin. It does not matter what their targets are because they will not get very far across our borders.'

There was silence. Kerim was beginning

to feel that he had made a mistake. Too many mistakes. His chair was hard and uncomfortable, and there was a throbbing pain starting up again behind his temples. Reinhard was watching him still without emotion, his square glasses reflecting flashes of light from the single bulb in the ceiling and hiding his eyes. Finally Reinhard said:

'What you have told me so far is of no value. There is nothing to make me feel indebted to you; nothing to persuade me to release the girl. What else can you tell me?'

'There is nothing else.' Kerim closed his eyes wearily, but after a moment opened them again. 'But I do not agree that what I have already told you is of no value. I gave you the details of those two training schools in good faith, and my information would have been important if you had not already known of them through George. And you have already said that I have done you a service by killing Rashid. You can repay that service by releasing Schererzade.'

He saw that Reinhard was not impressed

222

and his tone became angrier.

'Damn you, you even owe a direct favour to Schererzade herself. If you know the details of her previous career then you know that it was she who smuggled the filmed plans of Nasser's present military campaign against Israel out of Egypt. She was working then as an Israeli agent, and if I hadn't pulled her out of Cairo she would have been shot by the Egyptians as one of your spies!'

'That I do not dispute. But Schererzade initially gave the film of those plans to the British, and cost me the lives of some of my best agents in Egypt in trying to get them back. Now she returns as a double agent working for the British again. She changes sides just a little too often.'

'But she has never worked against you. She passed that film on to the British only because she had no choice. It was no fault of hers that your agents got themselves killed. She was almost dead herself in that hospital in Cairo. And in any case, the facts contained in those filmed documents were passed on to your people. They must have helped you to prepare for the present situation.'

'Perhaps.' The admission was not accompanied by any signs of weakening on Reinhard's part. 'But the debts we owe she has cancelled out. There is no reason why I should be lenient with her — unless of course you can strain your memory and find something else to give you a bargaining position. What can you tell me about British Military Intelligence, and your ex-employer, Major Jackson?'

Kerim said harshly, 'I didn't come here to betray my former employers. I'm not that kind of a traitor. I'll bargain anything I know that will help you against your Arab enemies, but nothing more.'

'You surprise me.' Reinhard sounded sincere. 'But what is there left that you can tell me about our enemies?'

Kerim said nothing, for he knew now that he had lost. He had no more to offer, and even if he was prepared to betray all that he knew about Jackson and British Intelligence he doubted now that Reinhard would grant him any favours. Reinhard watched him for almost a minute, and then he smiled.

'So, you have no more information. You come to ask for a deal, but you have nothing practical to exchange for this girl you desire so badly. Now it is my turn to offer a deal to you.'

Kerim stared at him in slow surprise. 'What kind of a deal?'

'To undertake a mission for me, in return for freedom for your friend Schererzade. You know Egypt and you know Cairo, you were born and raised there. Now you are an exile, but you still have contacts and you have already made one dangerous mission into Egypt to rescue this girl. You stole her away from the Egyptians and smuggled her out of the country to safety. You could perform a similar mission for me.'

'I don't understand you.'

'Then I shall explain more fully. Have you ever heard of a man named Otto Wolffe?'

Kerim was alert now. He said cautiously:

'I have heard the name. Wolffe is Egypt's pet Nazi spy-master. It was he who trained both Rashid and Barek. Jackson did mention that he was a wanted war criminal, and that your people would be eager to get hold of him.'

Reinhard's eyes glittered.

'Then you know what I am asking. Go back into Egypt and bring out Otto Wolffe. Bring him here to Israel to stand trial, and you can have the girl with my blessing.'

14

The Psychological Moment

Kerim felt suddenly cold, as though a chill and deathly wind had gently caressed the back of his neck. Reinhard's eyes were again hidden by the reflected light striking sharp flashes off his square-rimmed glasses, but the bleak set of his face showed that he was fully serious. He had hunched slightly forward over the desk, his shoulders curved and his chin lowered. Again the funeral atmosphere brooded around him.

Kerim said slowly and distinctly:

'What you ask is impossible. You already know that. Jackson told me that you've made attempts before to get Wolffe out of Egypt, suicide attempts that have done nothing but sacrifice good agents. And some of those agents must have known Cairo equally as well as myself. And in any case, you seem to have suddenly forgotten that there's a war brewing right on your doorstep. A few moments ago you were reminding me that Israel will soon be fighting for her life. Now you've got your priorities mixed. With the Arabs howling for your blood it's time to forget about old vendettas.'

Reinhard's mouth curled into its charade of a smile.

'Soiron, that is the whole point of my argument. The Arabs are supremely confident that they are going to exterminate us, to wipe Israel completely into the sea. Their transistor radios have told them so and they believe it, even their leaders believe it. Even before the battle they are convinced that Israel is finished, and it is they who have forgotten the old vendettas. I will admit that we have failed in previous attempts to kidnap Otto Wolffe and bring him back to Israel, but if ever he relaxes his guard it will be now. This is the time when he will not expect another attempt to be made, because Israel needs every single one of her sons to fight on the battlefield in her defence. Now is the psychological moment.'

228

Kerim said bluntly, 'It's also the psychological moment for any Israeli agent caught in Egypt to be literally torn to pieces by the mobs. You're asking me to commit suicide.'

'No.' Reinhard's head swayed from side to side like that of a lazy vulture. 'I am offering you an opportunity to save the girl. Her crimes are not great but my power is. In the present emergency I can have her shot — or I can have her released. The choice is yours.' He paused. 'You must love this girl very much. You rescued her from Cairo, and now you cut yourself off from your friends and risk your neck to come to me. Yes, my friend, I think you must have a great capacity for love.'

'And you have a great capacity for hate. What's so special about Wolffe? Is it because he's responsible for training so many Egyptian agents, or is it just the old, old story of participation in Hitler's answer to the Jewish problem?'

'It is both, but with Wolffe there is something more. Wolffe was a member of the SD, the elite security and foreign intelligence service set up by Heydrich's protége Schellenberg inside the SS. The task of the SD was to organize intelligence work outside Germany, planting agents behind the Russian lines and preventing counter Communist agents from penetrating into Germany and the occupied countries. In that organization Wolffe could, to a certain extent, have avoided the so-called Jewish problem. Instead he preferred to hunt Jews inside Germany. His choice was deliberate and he was hounding the Jews even before Hitler's final condemnation to the gas ovens. He hounded them for one simple reason — to prevent Schellenberg and the others from suspecting that he too had Semitic blood. Wolffe was the foulest of all traitors hunting his own kind. Otto Wolffe is a German Jew.'

Reinhard's voice had become more guttural and suddenly Kerim understood. He said flatly:

'And you also are a German Jew.'

'That is so.' Apart from the thickening of his voice Reinhard showed no emotion.

'I was one of the few who survived. Most of my family went to the gas ovens — sent there by Otto Wolffe. We called him the Black Wolf. His fear for his own life made him hate and destroy his own people. Now he no longer has to fear the Nazi leaders of the Third Reich, and instead he dreads Israeli vengeance. That is the principle reason why he works for Egypt, training their agents and spies and dedicating himself to the destruction of Israel.

'So you see, my friend, there are many reasons why we want this man. To make him stand trial for his war crimes, and to remove a present threat against the security of Israel. And now the time is ripe, and you are the man. You will bring Otto Wolffe out of Egypt.'

Kerim said sarcastically:

'And how am I going to achieve this miracle, which your own department has been unable to accomplish since 1945?'

'At the moment I am not sure.' Reinhard spoke frankly. 'Until a few hours ago when I was informed of your defection this plan had not occurred to

231

me. But you have contacts in Cairo, resources of your own. I too have agents there who will give you any help you require apart from actual participation in the kidnapping raid. At this time I cannot afford to lose them. I will repeat myself again and say that this is the psychological moment. You will have the advantage of surprise. The task should not be beyond you.'

'If it's to be a solo effort then it is beyond me. I can't do the impossible.'

'Then it is a pity that Schererzade will have to be shot. In a time of war spies cannot be tolerated.'

Again Kerim felt that dark, chill wind, like a shroud closing softly around him. For a long moment the room was absolutely silent and neither of them moved. Reinhard's face was sombre, like an undertaker waiting patiently before a grave.

'I will make a deal,' Kerim said at last. 'I can't bring Wolffe out of Egypt, but perhaps you are right about this being the psychological moment, I might be able to reach him inside Egypt. Kidnapping is out, but a kill might be possible.'

'But I want him alive!' Anger was Reinhard's first show of emotion. 'I want him alive, here in Israel, to stand trial before the whole world. And then I want him hanged where I can see it, where I can even pull the rope.'

Kerim said harshly, 'You want propaganda and you can't damn well have it. You had your fun with Eichmann, but this time you'll have to forgo the big show and be satisfied with a simple kill. I'll carry out the execution for you, but I can't do anything more.'

'A simple murder isn't enough. It's too good for a swine like Wolffe!'

'It's that or nothing. You'll never get him out for trial, not even now. You don't even have any kind of a plan, and you can only offer me a minimum of help. With you this is just a crazy impulse because the time is right and you think that you have the right lever to pitch me into Egypt. I'm just a tool you've found, a free gift, and it doesn't matter if I get chopped, you've still lost nothing. But I'm not prepared to commit pointless suicide, not even for Schererzade. You can continue to dream your glorious dreams of technicolour vengeance, or you can settle for a simple kill in cold black and white. The choice is yours.'

Reinhard glared at him, and then abruptly swivelled his chair and looked away. Kerim could sense the tension in the man as he watched the thin, black-clad shoulders, and he was aware that his own stomach muscles were knotted into a tight, tangled ball. For a full minute Reinhard silently considered, and then slowly he swung back to face Kerim across the desk. His spectacles glittered and his mouth was rigid. He seemed to have difficulty in speaking.

'All right, my friend, I will accept your offer. Execute Wolffe and the girl will be freed. But no tricks! I must be sure that Wolffe is dead. Across the back of his left hand there is a distinctive scar, a ragged zig-zag pattern across the knuckles. Bring me that hand so that I can check the scar and the fingerprints. It should not be difficult to sever it from the wrist once Wolffe is dead.'

Kerim said slowly, 'I may not get that close, or I may not have enough time. A quick clean kill is my only offer. I shall have to get out fast.'

'Bring me the hand,' Reinhard repeated. 'I must be certain that Wolffe is dead.'

Kerim felt a shiver prying into the knots in his stomach, and knew that Reinhard was a fanatic. The Israeli not only wanted proof of death, he wanted the dead man's hand as visible compensation for the loss of his desired propaganda trial. On the severed hand he could feast his eyes and his imagination, and allow it to replace the hanging he would not see. Kerim swallowed hard and then nodded his head.

'All right, it's a deal. When do I start?'

Reinhard twisted his mouth, his ugliest smile yet.

'We will wait a few days longer. The Arab armies face our frontiers but they have yet to rally their own morale. They will flex their muscles, and cry abuse and insults, and at the same time create incidents which they will term Israeli

235

provocation. There is time yet to make some preparation for your mission. The angry darkness of hatred is enveloping the tiny state of Israel, and blinding those who hate. Let them build up their hatred until it blinds them completely, and when the moment comes Israel will scatter their armies — and during the confusion of the war you will strike out Otto Wolffe. You will strike him dead and bring me that left hand with the zig-zag scar.'

★ ★ ★

It was the afternoon of the following day when Schererzade was taken from her cell. As yet she had suffered no ill-treatment during the four days since her arrest, but still there was a nervous tremor in her stomach as she was led through the cold, bare corridors of the prison. She had been questioned but not harshly interrogated, and she feared that the harsher interrogations were to come. Her jailers had told her nothing of why she had been summoned, and they were walking just a little too fast for her comfort. After being discharged from the hospital in Nicosia she had been left with a slight limp that was barely noticeable when she walked slowly, but now that she was being forced into haste it was showing.

She was taken into a small room with a minimum of furniture. Reinhard rose from behind a desk to greet her, and although his smile was meant to be pleasant the trembling in her stomach became more pronounced. He was a stranger to her, but intuition flashed one word into her mind. The Shinbeth. The officers who had arrested her had been efficient but not cold. This man she sensed was both cold and ruthless. Her escort was dismissed and nervously she passed her tongue over suddenly dry lips.

Reinhard offered her a chair, and then turned away and opened a connecting door that led into the next room. He said calmly:

'I will leave you for a few minutes. There is someone who wishes to speak with you privately.'

237

He went out and Kerim appeared in his place.

Schererzade stared, unable to speak as her emotions roared through a tumult of change. From fear to relief, through joy and love and alarm, and then skidding back again into a new and even more painful fear. It was Kerim, but there were faint but definite changes from the man she had known in Cyprus. The steel grey eyes were no longer quite so sharp and brilliant, and the ageless face had begun to reflect its years in blurred lines of tiredness. She stood up from her chair but could not move forward, and then found her voice.

'Kerim, oh no — they have taken you a prisoner also.'

Kerim realized then that his expression was not wholly reassuring. He had been given the opportunity to sleep since his first encounter with Reinhard, but too many thoughts and doubts about the task that lay ahead had helped to spoil his rest. He smiled quickly and went forward to meet her.

'No, Schererzade, I am not a prisoner.

238

And neither are you any more. You are leaving this place. You will go to a hotel where you will be under open arrest. You will have to report daily to the police, but it will only be for a few days, or weeks at the most. Then you will be really free.'

Her face was blank, bewildered, and at the same time filled with her still conflicting emotions. Her dark eyes searched his face, and he could feel her tremble as his hands gripped her shoulders. Reinhard had closed the door behind them and they were alone, and Kerim drew her more firmly into his arms. They kissed, and Schererzade forgot the intrigue that surrounded her as a captured spy and remembered painfully that she was a woman in love.

Her body was stronger now, and Kerim no longer had to fear that he would hurt her by holding her too close. Her heart was afraid and yearning and her mouth was a whimpering moan of delicious surrender. After a minute their embrace relaxed and Schererzade rested her cheek upon his shoulder. Slowly the harsher realities intruded and she pulled back a little to look up into his face once more.

'But, Kerim — I cannot understand. Why am I free? And if you are not a prisoner why are you here?'

He answered simply:

'I have defected. I brought some information to the Shinbeth to help them against the Arabs, and for that, and for a small service which I still have to perform, all the charges against you are to be dropped.'

'But, Kerim — ' There was uncertainty in her eyes. 'If you have defected then you can never return to work for Jackson. And the Israelies will never trust you fully. No one trusts a double spy. Perhaps — perhaps Jackson will even try to have you killed!'

'There is no reason that he should be so drastic. I have not betrayed Jackson, or at least I have done nothing that can harm him or his department. The information I traded was of general interest only.'

'I believe you, but can you be sure that Jackson will believe you? Changing sides is a dangerous game, you are risking your life.'

Kerim smiled bleakly. 'All of life is a risk, it is one long gamble from birth to death. And I could not stand by and let you rot in an Israeli jail.'

'You mean that you did this only for me?' There was disbelief and then sadness written into her dark but lovely face. 'Kerim, I am not worth it! You risk your life for a bint!'

Kerim's mind filtered back into the past, enlightening that last memory around her hospital bed in Nicosia. He said slowly:

'Is that why you accepted Jackson's job? Is that why you decided to come as a spy into Israel?'

She stared up at him miserably. 'But it was best, Kerim, it was the best thing for you. Do you know how I started my life as a dancer? I started by dancing stark naked in a filthy little side show in Port Said. Can you imagine how many men have gazed and gloated over my body? How many beds I have been in? How many lovers I have had?' Her voice edged towards bitter hysteria. 'Have you forgotten that I betrayed the Egyptian

Colonel who was my last lover? Did you know that for trusting me he has since been disgraced and imprisoned for his negligence?'

Kerim's hands tightened on her shoulders, silencing her by the digging pain of his fingers. He said harshly:

'I know all of that — but what kind of a man do you think I am, some kind of a saint? I have known my own fair share of women. Only three nights ago a girl died because I seduced her and used her. I enjoyed her body and picked her mind, and when I left her she had three bullets in her back.

'Schererzade, we are both in a dirty business. While we stay in it we cannot help being tainted by dirt. But we don't have to stay in it. In fact we both of us now have no choice but to get out. Neither of us is of any more use to the British, Arabs or Jews. Reinhard wants me to do just one job, but that's only because none of his own men will tackle it, there's nothing more after that. We're two of a kind.'

'But what is going to happen to us?

When you have bought my freedom, where will we go?'

'I don't know. I've still got to earn your freedom. Then we'll think about it.'

Her mouth seemed to tremble as she said:

'Kerim, please be careful.'

And then he was holding her close and kissing her again. The confusion of her mind blotted out all but her aching love, releasing all the helpless, pent-up longing of their separation. And now Kerim no longer had any doubts about his present course of action. They owed loyalties to no one but themselves in this present vicious and twisted circle, and if a death was the only price for her life then he was fully prepared to kill.

15

Across the Sinai

For the next few days Kerim was kept busy in learning everything that was known about Otto Wolffe, and he learned it well for his life would almost certainly depend upon it. The German had converted a large, palatial villa, once owned by an intimate friend of the despotic King Farouk, into the most efficient spy school in the Middle East, but here the curriculum was on a far more ambitious scale than the crude imitations organized by Rashid in Syria and Jordan. They were nursery schools, while this was a permanent and long established college of espionage. Commando raids for the purposes of murder and sabotage were only remote side issues to the main courses of study. Instead the emphasis was on the organization of spy cells in surrounding countries; the skills of

244

maintaining and operating a hidden wireless; the art of coding and decoding messages; of micro-photography, of how to obtain and forward information to a central source. More practical classes dealt with methods of communication and identification, and the passing of messages in public places; with how to shadow an enemy operator and how to lose a shadow. Self-defence, the use of small firearms, and the various means of killing swiftly with a knife or bare hands were the final basic lessons.

There were plans and details of the villa available and Kerim studied them closely. The location was south of Cairo along the west bank of the Nile. The villa was a two-storied building with over a dozen rooms, surrounded by a high-walled garden. Behind the villa was the Nile and on the remaining three sides the land had been cleared back to leave a wide circle of open ground. There were three gates breaching the ten foot high walls, the main gateway opening towards the Cairo-Luxor road, a side gate and a third gate facing the Nile where a landing stage and a diving board had been built beside the river.

Reinhard explained that the ground floor rooms were used for lectures and instruction, while the upper floor consisted of living quarters for staff and students. Wolffe had his own private suite and bathroom on the top floor overlooking the Nile, but worked from a central office on the ground floor. He had three permanent aides; one a wireless and cyphers expert, the second a professor in psychology, and finally a tough judo and physical training instructor borrowed from the army. All were Egyptians, and the latter doubled with the most proficient of each crop of students as Wolffe's bodyguard. The basement beneath the villa had been enlarged to make an underground firing range suitable for practice with revolvers and other small arms, but where familiarity with a rifle or any larger weapon was required the students were coached by military experts on an army firing range.

Kerim absorbed everything, studying

photographs and drawings and even a reconstructed model of the villa that occupied the whole surface of a large table. Then he turned his attention to a more personal study of the man he was meant to kill. Here some of his cold enthusiasm began to wane, for Wolffe's photograph showed a gentle but slightly harassed face that could more easily have belonged to some old and trusted family lawyer. In fact he had started life as a law student before being embroiled in the events of history and the Nazi machine. Now his hair was turning grey, for it was a recent photograph, and he did not look like a man who had hounded his own people into the gas ovens. In fact it would have helped if he had looked more like Reinhard, for Reinhard did have the physical appearance of a possible mass murderer. It was a pity, Kerim thought bitterly, that faces could not be in accordance with character. Life could be so much easier.

Reinhard was beside him as he studied the photograph, and he tried to hide his thoughts as he asked:

'What precautions does he take for his personal safety?'

Reinhard said calmly. 'In his headmaster's office on the ground floor he's copied a few examples from his old chief Schellenberg. Microphones everywhere, an alarm siren that can be activated and bring guards running at the press of a button, and two automatic machine guns built into his desk at cross angles so that the touch of another button can spray the whole room before him with bullets. We lost an agent that way whom we managed to infiltrate into the spy school. He tried a direct assassination and got cut to pieces. Wolffe also has alarm siren buttons placed at strategic points around his living quarters, but to the best of our knowledge no more machine guns. Although he does have a Luger holstered at his hip. There are half a dozen guards usually within call, armed with Russian-made machine pistols, and most of the students are similarly armed.

'The grounds are patrolled irregularly by the guards, and we also know that there's a high voltage live wire running along the top of the wall that encircles the grounds. It fried another of our men to a crisp when we tried to put a three-man team over the wall one night. The gates are electrified at night.'

Kerim listened with growing doubts and said sarcastically:

'And what makes you think that they'll switch off the current as soon as the war starts. Wolffe isn't going to feel so secure that he'll get conscientious about saving electricity!'

Reinhard chuckled. 'No, we do not expect that. But his guards will relax their vigilance, they will be more interested in the war news coming through their transistors, and we have devised a means of getting you safely over the wall. Our next step is to put you through a stiff programme of training. We have found a similar villa which we have fitted with the kind of defences you can expect, so you can make as many dummy runs as you wish before you tackle the real thing. There is still time.'

★ ★ ★

There was in fact a full ten days of international bickering, during which Egypt blockaded the Gulf of Aqaba and mined the Straits of Tiran, Israel's only route of exit to the Red Sea. The massive build-up of the Arab armies continued, the United Nations argued within itself, and the super-powers jostled frantically for any scraps of position or prestige that might be won or lost by the actions of their chosen favourites. In a prolonged glory of cliff-hanging drama the Middle East balanced on the edge of war, and then on the 30th of May Egypt's President Nasser and King Hussein of Jordan signed a noisy defence pact that finally committed Jordan's army to the coming conflict, and formed the last support for a united Arab front.

When the news was heard Reinhard deemed that the time was ripe to launch Kerim into Egypt.

★ ★ ★

Within a matter of hours the two men were seated in a small jeep driving fast across the Negev desert towards the Egyptian frontier. The sands appeared empty but Kerim noted the innumerable track patterns of the heavy tanks that had moved forward to take up their battle positions during the preceding weeks. The sun was scorching and the air was filled with dust, and he did not envy the men who would soon have to sweat and fight from within their lumbering steel fortresses.

The drive ended beside a small encampment of nomads who had pitched their few tents beside a desert well. The jeep skidded to a stop and the driver remained at the wheel while both Kerim and Reinhard got out. The men who waited silently as they approached were Bedouin Arabs, fierce independent tribesmen wearing flowing desert robes, their arrogant faces burnt the colour of dark oak by the sun. They were a small party, perhaps a score of men with their women children and camels.

Reinhard said softly, 'They owe

allegiance to no one but themselves. They roam as they please. Their loyalty cannot be bought but their services can.'

Kerim said nothing. He too was wearing long desert robes and a white head-dress secured by a black cord, and he felt self-conscious. The Bedouin had recognized a stranger in their own clothes.

There was a brief parley between Reinhard and the chief of the Bedouin, while Kerim patiently waited. Everything had been previously arranged and it was only a matter of exchanging courtesies and the necessary payment. Finally Reinhard shook hands, wished Kerim luck and returned to his jeep. A moment later the jeep was speeding back through a cloud of dust towards Tel Aviv, and Kerim was left in the hands of the nomads.

There was practically no delay. The Bedouin chief was a curt old man who issued a string of orders. Six of his tribesmen hurried to round up their camels, a spare beast was saddled for Kerim and they were ready to move.

There were no friendly introductions for this was purely a business transaction. Within half an hour of parting from Reinhard Kerim was riding south towards the Sinai with a mounted escort.

Night came, and under the cover of darkness they threaded through both the Israeli and Egyptian battle lines. The old chieftain knew the desert as a child knows its mother's face, and not once were they challenged. The sky was bright with stars as they guided their lurching camels through the hills and dunes, and it seemed as though the hostile desert had swallowed up the vast armies that were poised here to hurl themselves into the third Arab-Israeli war. Then, shortly after midnight, the old chieftain raised a hand to stop the silent column in its tracks. He pointed through a gap in the hills, and below them Kerim saw great ramparts of Russian-built Egyptian tanks and field guns all facing towards Israel. The lines of armour vanished into the dark shrouded horizon, threatening and waiting.

The tiny caravan continued on its

cautious way, alert for patrols, alert for land mines, and frequently twisting and doubling back. A lifetime in the desert had sharpened the night sight and hearing of the old man in the lead, and it seemed to Kerim that he could actually scent danger before it appeared. He knew that the many changes of direction were made to avoid troop encampments and patrols, but he saw no more actual evidence of their existence. Towards dawn the caravan quickened its pace, heading directly out across the Sinai, and Kerim realized that they were through the opposing armies. He was just a little relieved that the war had not chosen to erupt while they were squarely in the middle.

At noon they stopped where a few pathetic date palms huddled around a desert well. They ate and then slept and sheltered through the burning heat of the afternoon, and then mounted up and rode on again at dusk. They were avoiding all roads and main routes, and although they several times heard the distant rumble of more tanks and armour heading for the front they saw nothing.

The second day was similar to the first, and on the third night they reached the silent barrier of the Suez Canal, like a deep, black sword slash cutting cleanly across their path. To their left, beyond the canal glowed the faint lights of the Egyptian town of Ismailia mid-way between Suez and Port Said. Here Kerim was obliged to part from his escort, and after brief goodbyes and a grudging *shalom* the Bedouin wheeled away and rode swiftly back into the desert, leading Kerim's riderless camel in their wake. Alone Kerim turned to face the canal.

He stripped naked and then tied his ordinary clothes and a few oddments, which now included a sharp throwing knife and his own .38 automatic, into a bundle. The flowing outer robes he had worn for the desert crossing he no longer needed, and these he buried in the sand. Then he moved carefully down the slope of the canal bank into the cool dark water and swam across to the far side, pushing his bundle ahead of him. The far bank was an awkward, difficult climb but eventually he reached the top.

After he had dried and dressed he began the long walk into Ismailia, where the railway line connected with Cairo.

16

The Empty Room

Kerim arrived in Cairo on the afternoon of the second day in June, hot, sweating and dirty and cursing the chaotic discomfort of Egypt's over-crowded railway. The train journey had been a long one, his carriage had been bursting at the seams with noisy, squabbling Arab peasants, and he ached in every muscle. The three nights of sitting astride a bad tempered camel in the Sinai had been an easier ordeal.

Cairo, the city of his birth, had changed little since his last memories. It was still an old city, divided by the Nile, with its modern quarters and new buildings made grubby by its inhabitants. If anything there seemed to be more people in the bustling streets, and they were noisier and more jubilant than ever before. There was war fever in the air, and premature grins for their promised victory. Transistor radios blared the news that Russian warships had entered the Mediterranean to support the Arab states, and the first clash of fighting had already occurred on the Israel and Syrian frontier. Cairo was confident, eager for blood, and thriving upon hatred for Israel. The atmosphere made Kerim shiver.

Reinhard had given him the address of a café in the bazaars near the old market area of Khan-El-Khalili, and he made his way there by foot from the station. He was shabbily dressed in trousers, shirt and jacket and did not wish to draw attention to himself by taking a taxi, while the bulging buses that went past were even more over-crowded than the train had been.

He found the café in a narrow, smelling street and went inside. A few customers sipped mint tea and gossiped around the cheap, marble-topped tables, and there was a counter with the inevitable coffee machine. His parents had owned a café such as this before his father had died, and there was a faint taste of home-sickness. His exile had made him lose contact with his mother and now he did not even know if she were alive. If she was then she must certainly believe him to be dead. Life was savage and the past could not be changed. He pushed it out of his mind.

He went up to the counter and ordered a coffee. The man who served him was short and heavy, with a soft face and curling hair. Kerim was reminded sourly of George in Damascus. He paid for the coffee in Egyptian piastres, provided by Reinhard, and then asked:

'Can I speak to Daniel?'

The soft face stayed blank, but the voice was cautious and hard. Kerim realized that his first assessment had been wrong, and that this man was in a totally different class from his Syrian host.

'Who is asking?'

'My name is Soiron. That should be enough. I believe that I am expected.'

The soft face watched him for a moment, and then nodded.

'Come this way.'

Kerim followed him up a flight of stairs to a room above the café. Two men were inside, one a thin youth in his teens who sat before a table, prying doubtfully into the entrails of a transistor radio with a screwdriver; the other was an older man who relaxed full length on an unmade bed. Both looked up as the door was opened. Soft-face said flatly:

'A visitor. His name is Soiron, he asks for Daniel.'

The man on the bed stretched lazily and then stood up. His white shirt was open to the waist and he looked tough and casual. His smile was a flickering movement at the corners of his mouth as he folded his arms across his chest. He studied Kerim for a moment, and then admitted:

'I am Daniel.'

Kerim said slowly, 'I think you have the other half of this.'

He held out a torn Egyptian banknote, feeling self-conscious and over-dramatic. There had to be some means of identification and this was the simplest routine, even though it was out-dated.

Daniel's mouth flickered with more amusement as he took the note, but he did not bother to check it. Instead he shredded it into smaller pieces and dropped it into a waste-paper basket.

'So you are from Reinhard,' he said calmly. 'We have been told about you. We know what you intend to do. The things you need are all ready for you, and you can stay here until you have made your attempt. But if things go wrong do not endanger this café, stay away from us. You understand?'

Kerim understood. These men were permanent agents of the Shinbeth, and no doubt they had been part of the previous attempts that had failed to reach Otto Wolffe. Now they were obeying orders from Reinhard, but only reluctantly. He was a danger to them and they did not even want him to succeed. Any co-operation that he received would be minimal, and he could sense the resentment and hostility that brooded in the room. He felt like cursing Reinhard but knew that that would not help, he had to make the best of it and then get out. He faced Daniel and said harshly:

'I think you've made yourself clear. I want some food and then a bed for the night. Tomorrow night I'll do the job.'

★ ★ ★

Kerim slept badly, ate poorly and was tense throughout the following day. Daniel had deliberately made himself absent, the soft-faced man was running the café, and Kerim was left with only the youth for company in the upstairs room. The boy had repaired his radio and played it endlessly, filling the room with screeching music interrupted by hate-filled Arab news broadcasts full of the fervour of the coming war. In the afternoon Kerim finally lost his temper and forcibly switched off the radio. The boy protested almost dangerously, showing an unexpected streak of viciousness, but then decided to take his radio downstairs into the café. Kerim thankfully lay down on the bed and tried to catch a few more hours of sleep.

It was night when he awoke. Daniel

had returned, and already it was time for him to move. He had decided against a preliminary reconnoitre, partly because it was an extra risk that offered no real advantage, for he had faith in Reinhard's briefing, and partly because he was anxious to be finished with the whole business. Haste could be dangerous, but there had been almost two weeks in Israel to prepare, and any further delay would not affect his chances of success or failure.

Daniel had provided a car, and grudgingly offered himself as a guide and driver. The other two men remained behind. Kerim's stomach was faintly queasy as he dressed in black trousers, a black woollen sweater and rubber-soled shoes. The flat-handled throwing knife fitted into a special sheath that lay between his shoulder-blades, secured by a thin strap that passed over his right shoulder, across his chest and under his left arm. The hilt was within easy reach of his fingertips and he could draw the knife from behind his shoulder and throw it accurately in the same move.

His automatic was holstered at his waist just before his left hip and there was a silencer in his pocket, but these he hoped that he would not have to use. Even a silenced gun made a soft cough, and only the knife was wholly soundless.

It was after midnight when they drove south out of Cairo along the Luxor road. The Nile banks were fertile with palm and banana groves making black, feathered patterns against the night. There were darkened fields and crude mud and stone villages and buildings. A few more elaborate villas. Daniel drove silently. There was no friendship between them, and no trust.

They passed their destination. The villa was obscured by tall, slanting palms that shielded it from the road and Daniel drove by without slackening speed, speaking for the first time to point out the location. After a quarter of a mile the Shinbeth man stopped, and then looked directly at Kerim.

'I will leave you here, and then drive on. It is too dangerous to wait.' He glanced at his watch. 'I will give you two hours. That should be enough — one way or another. Then I will drive back this way again and pick you up. If you are not here I shall drive straight back to Cairo. You must realize that I cannot afford to endanger my own position, not for personal reasons but because my services are important to Israel, especially so at this present moment.'

Kerim nodded and checked the time by his watch. It was one-thirty a.m. He retrieved the small rucksack containing the items of equipment he needed from the back of the car and got out, slipping his arms into the straps. Daniel hesitated before reluctantly wishing him success, and then the car sped off along the darkened road. Kerim watched it disappear and wondered grimly whether Daniel really did intend to return.

He had to call to memory the picture of Schererzade's lonely, and frightened face, and remember that if he backed out of their bargain then Reinhard would most certainly have her shot. Only Schererzade was important now, and after a moment he steeled himself to turn and walk back towards the villa.

★ ★ ★

It was exactly like the reconstructed model he had studied at the Shinbeth HQ in Tel Aviv. He approached it through the palm trees along the bank of the Nile, and then lowered himself on to his belly to wriggle the last few yards up to the edge of the wide open space that had been cleared around the outer walls. All was peaceful and still, there was no wind to stir the palm fronds and only the Nile moved, flowing silently and almost unnoticeably towards the great delta beyond Cairo. It was a dark night, with few stars and no moon.

Kerim freed his automatic and screwed on the long nose of the silencer, wishing now that he had something heavier, a .45 or even a machine pistol. This first step was the most crucial of all, for only luck and a fast run could take him across the open space to the outer wall. There was absolutely no cover. For fifteen minutes he watched and waited, and now the tension had eased from his body. Cold determination was needed now, and he willed that quality into every nerve and muscle. When he was sure that he was not being observed he rose to his feet and swiftly made his run.

The distance was fifty yards. The rucksack hampered him and the soft sand dragged at his feet. He moved in a fast, crouching zig-zag in case he was met by a stutter of bullets and his heart was pounding as he skidded to a stop in the black shadow thrown by the wall. He half-knelt, ready for immediate flight if the alarm was raised, but the villa remained wrapped in silence. The run had taken twelve seconds but he had not been seen.

He listened for a full minute and then lowered the automatic. Quickly he unslung the rucksack and opened it, arranging the contents on the sand. There were five two-foot sections of a light-weight collapsible ladder which he fitted together with practised fingers and leaned against the ten-foot wall. The rungs were just wide enough for him to insert one foot at a time, but despite its flimsy appearance the ladder was quite strong enough to bear his weight. The rucksack also contained two thick rubber shields shaped to fit the top of the wall.

Kerim swiftly climbed the ladder. Along the top of the wall was a fine mesh of copper netting, earthed at intervals to act as a conductor to the high voltage live wire that was strung along tiny insulated posts some two inches high. To touch both meant a lethal electric shock, an instantaneous death. Kerim's eyes were level with that slender glimmer of evil as he checked that the garden beyond was empty. There was no sign of the guards and the villa remained undisturbed. Kerim drew a deep breath, steadying his balance on the ladder as he gingerly inched one of the rubber shields between the earthed copper mesh and the live wire. It fitted firmly into place over the mesh and the top of the wall, and Kerim swallowed hard when the job was done. Next, just as carefully, he placed the second rubber shield in position over the first, sandwiching and insulating a two foot length of the wire.

He wiped the sweat from his face and then climbed higher up the ladder and straddled the wall, sitting on the rubber cushion he had made with the unchecked current still flowing harmlessly beneath him. He drew up the ladder, passed it over the wall and wriggled it into a solid position on the inside. Then he climbed swiftly down into the villa grounds. The automatic came out into his hand as his feet touched earth and for a moment he kept low, bringing the ladder down to lay flat against the foot of the wall behind him. The whole exercise had been performed as smoothly as the dummy runs he had made in Israel, and still there was no alarm being raised inside the villa.

There was no sign of the guards, and that worried him. Reinhard had said that there would be irregular patrols. However, there was no time to waste and he moved cautiously forward, alert for trip wires or any other kind of a trap. The silenced automatic was in his left hand now, leaving his right free to reach above his shoulder for the hilt of the knife. If it became necessary he would use the knife first. Only if there was no time would he risk the muffled cough of the gun.

He circled to the side of the villa, and here was the drain-pipe that was to provide him with a route to the flat roof. Hesitation meant failure, speed was his only hope, and so he went up fast. They had clocked him at eight seconds during his best practice run, but this time he was sure that he had trimmed another second. He was also only just in time to escape the two guards who wandered round the corner of the villa with machine pistols cradled loosely in their arms. He crouched high above them to watch for a moment, but they had no suspicions and were clearly making a routine check. He waited until they had returned to the front of the villa, and then crossed the roof to the back of the building that overlooked the Nile.

He stopped directly above the bedroom where Wolffe would be sleeping, and felt the nervous tension loosening his bowels and crawling back into his stomach. So far everything had gone perfectly, but beyond this point he was on his own without the well-remembered drill of the past practice runs to sustain him. Now it was the real thing. He had to kill his man, and in his pocket there was even a plastic bag to carry away the severed left hand that Reinhard demanded as proof of death. The killing would be bad enough, but the grisly deed that would have to follow was already making him feel sick.

He had to think again of Schererzade, and he was glad that he had not told her all of what he was expected to do as the price of her life.

He went on because it was now too late to turn back. The balcony that led into Wolffe's bedroom was immediately below him, and reassured by utter silence he lowered himself carefully over the edge of the roof. He hung at arm's length and when he dropped it was only a matter of twelve inches before his rubber-soles smacked lightly against the balcony floor.

He pressed quickly against the wall, and again his heart was hammering until he was sure that the sound had not been heard.

Once more the silenced automatic was in his left hand, and with his right he gently tried the tall french windows. They were not locked and he had the sudden disturbing thought that this last stage was becoming too easy. He searched for tell-tale wires that might have led to an alarm bell, remembering Reinhard's warning about press-button sirens, but he could see nothing. He had to gamble now and holding his breath he inched open the windows. There was no frantic ringing of bells, no flashing lights and no nightmare of bullets crashing into his body, and slowly he relaxed. He eased into the bedroom and stood behind the curtains.

The fingers of his right hand found the knife and slipped it free, turning it and balancing the blade in the palm of his hand. He listened for the sound of breathing that would mark the position of the sleeping man, and he had already decided upon a hard, silent throw to the threat. Even in darkness he was confident of his ability, for in the past two weeks he had repeatedly practised throwing blindfolded at a sound. It was cold-blooded murder, but he could not think of that. Think instead of the Jewish blood that dripped from the hands of Otto Wolffe. Think of Schererzade.

He waited, listening, but there was no sound; absolutely no sound at all.

The darkness became cold, snakes curled in his stomach, and now he was really afraid. He finally moved the curtains gently to one side with the long, silenced barrel of the automatic, but he could see nothing.

The room was filled with darkness, but there was no sound of breathing, and slowly he realized that it was empty. There was no one there, neither Otto Wolffe nor anyone else.

17

Torture

The time was three-thirty a.m. precisely when the car returned to the rendezvous. Daniel slowed it to a stop and Kerim appeared swiftly from the shadows, scrambling inside and slamming the door. Daniel wasted no time on words but gunned the engine and drove on quickly towards Cairo. Kerim pushed the awkward rucksack down on to the floor between his knees and said bitterly:

'Don't sweat. I haven't started any panic.'

The Shinbeth man relaxed enough to look at him.

'What happened? Did you kill Wolffe?'

Kerim said savagely, 'Wolffe wasn't there. It was all too damned easy, the guards were slack because there was nobody there to guard. According to your damned clever Reinhard Wolffe

274

never leaves the school, he's too scared to come outside the walls. But this time Reinhard was wrong. All I found was an empty room.'

Daniel was driving normally now, leaning back in his seat as he handled the car. Passing shadows thrown by the tall, dark palms rushed across his face, blurring any expression he might have had. His voice was calm, casual.

'Did you search beyond the bedroom?'

'I checked the bedroom and the bathroom, that was all. The bed had been stripped. There were half a dozen suits in the wardrobe, but also there were several empty hangers. There was no toothpaste or shaving kit in the bathroom, so all the indications are that he's left the villa for a few days.'

Daniel's smile flickered.

'That is a pity. But very convenient for you.'

Kerim tightened his mouth and no more was said during the last few miles of the drive back to Cairo. They crossed the Nile by the El Giza Bridge, avoiding the city centre where during the day the sandbag barricades had been going up around the government buildings, and where the Egyptian police were most thickly clustered with their machine pistols. Daniel knew Cairo well and used the back streets to circle round to Khan-El-Khalili. There was just enough room to drive the car up the narrow street that led to the café, and Daniel parked immediately before the closed shutters.

They used a side entrance and went straight up to the room above the café where Daniel's colleagues, or underlings, waited. Formal introductions had never been made, and so Kerim had mentally christened the remaining two Shinbeth men as the Boy and the Ball. The Ball, the heavy, soft-faced man who ran the café, stood up as they entered, ignoring Kerim but looking enquiringly at Daniel.

'Another miss.' Daniel answered the unspoken question. 'Wolffe was out.'

The Ball looked at each man in turn.

'Are you sure that Soiron went in?'

Kerim glared at him contemptuously. 'If you had the nerve to try it yourself I would take that as an insult. Instead it is just a pathetic noise.'

There was a hostile silence. The soft face did not change but the eyes were steady and the Ball's body seemed to balance and freeze. The Boy filtered forward into Kerim's range of vision and he knew the Boy carried a knife. He was not sure about the Ball. There was an instinctive urge to step to one side so that he could watch all three of them at the same time but that would have been too theatrical. Melodrama made him feel foolish. Then Daniel moved forward and sat nonchalantly with one haunch on the table.

'Don't squabble,' he admonished. 'I don't doubt that Soiron went into the villa. The point is, what happens now?' He gazed at Kerim. 'What is your next move?'

Kerim said bluntly, 'That's entirely up to you. I came here to do a job and if I can locate Wolffe I'll still do it, or at least have another try. But I can't find him alone. If you still want no part of this business then I might as well pack up and go back to Israel.'

Daniel was silent, thinking hard, and Kerim could guess at the train of his thoughts. There was still resentment and distrust, and the reluctance to become involved, and yet at the same time the Shinbeth man could not openly refuse to co-operate, not unless he was prepared to defy Reinhard and accept the consequences.

The two satellites watched without offering advice, and their quarrel with Kerim was temporarily forgotten. All three of them were almost certainly Jews, but they were Middle Eastern Jews with no direct link to Europe and the concentration camps. They had no personal feeling of revenge towards Wolffe and his war crimes. They worked either for pay or for a future retirement to their national homeland. They too stood to be torn to pieces by the mobs if their loyalties were discovered during the present crisis, and he would not have blamed them if they had refused him any further help. It all depended upon how strongly they were controlled by the unseen shadow of Reinhard.

Daniel finally looked up and said grudgingly:

'We will do what we can. You will stay here in this room and keep out of sight, while we try to find out what has happened to Wolffe.'

★ ★ ★

That fourth day in June was the longest that Kerim could remember. The café was kept closed and shortly before noon Daniel and his two companions left on an errand which they did not explain. Kerim had been warned not to leave the room above the café during their absence and so he could only fret and wait in the close, stuffy heat of what was almost a prison cell. He tried to sleep on the bed but failed. There was a single window that looked down on to a busy section of street, but he tired of listening to the noise and watching the erratic flow of movement. The Boy had left his radio behind and he tuned it hopefully, but all he could get was the arrogant voice of Nasser proclaiming that the blockade of the Gulf of Aqaba would continue, and that the United Arab Republic was ready to crush any Israeli aggression. He switched it off in disgust and flopped down again on the bed. Frustration was eating into him again, and there was nothing to do but prowl the confines of his cage and wonder what Daniel and his satellites were planning. It was midnight before they returned to provide him with the answer.

He had at last been able to doze as the day cooled into night, and the sound of the returning car roused him from a shallow sleep. He stood up from the bed and crossed to the window, but the street below was empty, and from this angle he could not see the front of the café where the car had stopped. He waited, and it seemed that they were taking a long time, and then he heard clumsy movements on the stairs. There were quick footsteps and then the Boy appeared. He switched on the light, for Kerim had been standing in darkness, and then flashed his teeth in a nervous grin. There was no acknowledgement as he hurried across the room to close the wooden shutters outside the window, but then Kerim's attention was fixed on Daniel who followed the Boy into the room.

There was a long, struggling human bundle clamped firmly across the Shinbeth man's shoulder. It was enveloped in a long, coarse brown sack secured by a mess of rope and only a feeble wriggling movement showed that it was alive. Daniel strode across the room, hitched his shoulder forward, and dumped his burden on the bed. The sack twisted and the bound legs protruding from the open end kicked helplessly. Daniel stood back and casually flexed his arms and shoulder muscles, and then the Ball appeared behind him and closed the door.

All three of them looked very satisfied with themselves, and Kerim counted three smiles awaiting his response. He said blankly:

'What — or who, is that?'

Daniel said calmly, 'She is the best

281

that we can manage at such short notice, but I think she may be able to tell us where Wolffe has gone. She works as a maidservant at the villa, making beds and cleaning out the bathrooms for Wolffe and his three aides. The students have to look after themselves. She lives outside the villa and we picked her up on her way home. We wanted one of the students or guards but none of them showed. We could not hang about for too long in the area so we grabbed her while the opportunity was there and bundled her into the car.' He shrugged. 'Perhaps she is the better catch. Her absence will not be noticed so quickly.'

'Even so, you're taking a very big risk!'

Daniel shrugged again. 'Sometimes we have to take risks. I did not think that you would succeed in entering the villa to kill Wolffe. Perhaps I underestimated your capabilities, but that is not important now. We know that Wolffe has left his closely-guarded refuge, and if we can find out where he has gone there may be a real chance to finish him for good. That will get Reinhard off my back. If he keeps on sending agents here on suicide missions like yours he will kill us all. Reinhard is a maniac and there will be no peace for us while Wolffe lives. So, if there is a definite possibility of eliminating Wolffe it is worth the risk.'

Kerim looked at the now-still bundle on the bed and said slowly:

'Then you had better uncover her face, otherwise she will suffocate.'

Daniel gave him a curious stare, and then he turned to the radio that stood upon the table, switched it on and turned up the volume, filling the room with noisy Arab music. Even at that hour of night the sound of radio music was common as the people of Cairo sat up and listened eagerly for news broadcasts of the impending war, so the sound would not arouse suspicion. Also it would muffle any other sounds. Daniel nodded his head in time to the rhythm for a moment, and then glanced at the bed. He made an affirmative nod towards the Ball.

The soft-faced man came forward and

deftly produced a knife. The blade easily severed the outer ropes and then the Boy helped him to pull the long sack from the girl's head. She squirmed helplessly and Kerim saw that her hands were tied behind her back, while strips of white tape covered her eyes and her mouth. She could neither see nor speak.

Daniel gently pushed the Boy aside. He said quietly:

'We are going to ask you some questions. If you tell us the answers then we shall not have to hurt you. I am going to pull the tape away from your mouth, but please do not be childish enough to scream. No one will hear you, and you will be instantly punished. Do you understand?'

The girl lay motionless on the bed, her body rigid except for the frightened movement of her breasts. She made no sign that she had heard, but after a moment Daniel pulled slowly at the lower strip of white tape. The girl whimpered as it came away from her lips.

The Boy and the Ball watched with interest.

Kerim had a cold, hollow feeling in his stomach.

Daniel said calmly, 'That's better. Now you can talk. You are aware that Otto Wolffe has left the villa where you are employed. It was almost certainly you who stripped his bed to air it while he is away. Tell us, please, where he has gone? And for how long will he be absent?'

The girl's mouth twisted, but no words came out, only a choking sound and a sob.

Daniel waited, and then said:

'Answer please.'

The girl turned her face away and her mumble of words was too low for Kerim to distinguish. However, Daniel recognized their meaning and sighed almost sadly.

'I cannot believe you. I think that you do know the answer.'

He left the girl and half sat upon the table, reaching for the radio and turning the hideous wail of Arab music even higher. Then he folded his arms across his chest and nodded to the Ball. The soft-faced man used both hands to smooth back his curling black hair, as though preparing himself for a special appointment. He studied his victim reflectively and then he struck her two savage, cutting blows across the face with the back of his hand. The girl cried out as her head was rolled back and forth and tried to wriggle her tightly-bound body away from him across the bed. The Boy joined in to shut off her screams with his hand clamping brutally across her mouth, and then the Ball caught the top of her dress in both fists and ripped it open to her navel, baring her desperately heaving breasts. Daniel was calmly lighting himself a cigarette.

Kerim said tautly:

'She's probably telling the truth. Do we have to go in for the rough stuff?'

Daniel turned slowly to face him, and now the Shinbeth man looked fully hostile. The other two had hesitated and were waiting. Daniel said coldly:

'If she knows anything she will tell us. It is simply a matter of softening her resistance. If she does not know anything then that is a pity, but no further loss on our part. If you are squeamish you may go downstairs and wait in the café. We can manage quite capably without you.'

Kerim realized that all three were against him. Daniel alone was probably his own equal. The Ball was wary and watchful, and the Boy full of nervous excitement, coupled with a vicious streak. The odds were too much, but at least he didn't have to watch. He said sourly:

'All right, I'll wait below.'

He turned away and was aware of the scornful grins that were exchanged between the Boy and the Ball. Only Daniel refrained from any outwards signs of triumph.

Kerim closed the door behind him and slowly descended the darkened stairs. He switched on the light inside the café and stood for a moment, staring at the silent, empty tables. Music from the radio filtered down loudly from above but he could hear nothing else. It was all left to his imagination. He tried to shut his mind and moved deliberately behind the counter. His throat was dry and he opened a bottle of ice-cold beer from the refrigerator. It was bitter, the worst beer he had ever tasted.

Minutes passed. A muffled, gurgling scream sounded faintly through the straining tones of the Arab singer who now dominated the radio, causing Kerim to tighten his grip around his glass and swallow hard. The girl was simply a source of information; a nameless quality who meant nothing. He had to forget that she must have a personality, emotions and a soul. Forget that she was somebody's sister, or daughter, or lover.

A lover. *Schererzade!*

Her face floated into his mind and he realized that this could so easily have happened to Schererzade, she too had been a prisoner of the Shinbeth. Personalities and feelings meant nothing to these people, for the end always justified the means.

It came again. A definite scream. A long-drawn shriek of vibrant agony that clearly pierced the deafening blare of the radio. He could see its violent contortions written across Schererzade's face, and the violated body arched in pain was no longer that of a stranger but one that he knew. And then Dalia appeared again to haunt him, accusing him with dead eyes that would not stay closed. Dalia and Schererzade, the dead and the living, with their faces mingled together and reflecting the screaming agony of the nameless little Arab girl who was being tortured in the room above him.

The third series of screams cracked him open, shattering one form of resolve and hardening another. He set his glass down upon the counter and pulled the .38 automatic from its holster at his waist. His hands were steady as he reached into his pocket for the long, fat nose of the silencer and screwed it into place on the gun barrel. Then slowly he returned up the darkened staircase.

The screaming had stopped and the radio was now pouring out reedy and hysterical flute music. Kerim did not hesitate before the closed door, but pushed it open with his free hand. The radio drowned the slight noise he made and he had a brief moment to survey the changed scene.

The girl now lay huddled on the floor, either because she had fallen or had been thrown from the bed. The white strip of tape still blinded her eyes and her hands were still tied behind her back, but now she was naked. There was bright red blood showing between her legs, even though her knees were drawn up to her belly, and there was more blood staining her dark breasts where the nipples had been crushed. The three men stood in a half circle around her.

They sensed Kerim's presence and their heads turned, and only the Boy failed to notice the automatic in Kerim's hand. His face was pale and shiny with sweat, but he smiled as he said:

'We have the information. Wolffe has gone to Jordan. That is all she knows.'

18

War

The Boy's voice suddenly tailed off as he realized what was happening, the radio screeched on unconcerned and the only other sound was the whimpering moans from the girl on the floor. The Ball turned very slowly, his soft face still a little pansyish, but his eyes were freezing. The Boy held a knife but now he did not know what to do with it. The initial danger would come from Daniel.

Daniel was again wearing his white shirt open to the waist, standing perfectly balanced with his feet apart and his hands resting loosely by his thighs. His expression was enquiring and faintly amused, hardening on to his lean face. Kerim could sense his cool brain calculating the odds.

Unexpectedly the radio went dead.

The sharp silence was as startling as

a scream, and involuntarily all four men in the room glanced towards the table where the wailing chaos of flutes and drums had so abruptly ceased. Faint rustling sounds came from the radio, and imperceptibly the tension mounted. They had waited so long and now a swift flash of instinct made them forewarned. Their own antagonism, the pain-wrecked girl on the floor, the gun in Kerim's hand; all were forgotten. And then it came.

The excited tones of the announcer boomed in an almost deafening gabble that shook the room.

'Here is a special announcement. Early this morning the bandit state of Israel made a deliberate, savage, pre-planned aggression against the United Arab Republic. We are replying with all our strength. Our tanks and our soldiers are smashing into Israel. Our air force is destroying the bandit air force in the skies. Allah is with us. Victory is ours . . . '

There was more, but nobody was listening. After an eternity of brinkmanship the black clouds of hate had at last burst asunder. Arabs and Jews had plunged into the bloodbath and the Middle East was at war.

Slowly their attention returned to their own situation, but the news had acted as an escape valve and now the tension had dropped. Kerim had not moved from the doorway and still held the automatic to cover the three Shinbeth men. The Boy looked uncertain and the Ball waited for a lead from Daniel. Finally Daniel relaxed and walked over to the table. He picked up the radio and switched off the jubilant flow of Arabic that was now crowing a list of victories impossible for a war that had only just started. Silence descended upon the room again, and then he turned to face Kerim.

'Relax, Soiron. Obviously you came up here to stop what we were doing, but it is over, we already have all the information the girl can give. None of us can afford a shooting match here, and there are other things that are more important. Put the gun away and we will forget this intrusion.'

Kerim remained motionless and asked coldly:

'And what will happen to the girl?'

Daniel looked down at the huddled body on the floor and considered for a moment. Then he glanced at the Ball.

'Lift her back on to the bed and untie her hands. Get hot water and bandages and do what you can for her. We may have to keep her for a few days, but there is no need for any further ill treatment. Make sure she is as comfortable as possible.' He turned back to Kerim and finished. 'She has not seen our faces, and cannot lead anyone back to this place, so I think we can afford to dump her alive.'

Kerim had no faith in Daniel's promises, but for the moment he could see no alternative but to accept the Shinbeth man's word. The underlings were already carrying out their orders to lift the girl back on to the bed, and after a moment of hesitation Kerim lowered his automatic.

Daniel watched him unscrew the silencer and the corners of his mouth flickered faintly. He said:

'Let us go below. We have to talk.'

Kerim was wary, and allowed the

Shinbeth man to precede him down the stairs. The light was still on in the café and Daniel sat down casually before one of the white-topped tables, leaning forward on his elbows. Kerim sat down and faced him. Daniel said calmly:

'What we have learned is that Wolffe left Cairo forty-eight hours ago. The girl says he flew to Jordan, but he didn't pass through the International airport or I would have known. That means a private flight, probably from a military airfield. She doesn't know why he has gone or when he will be back, but he took with him two highly trained agents; the best of the current crop of Egyptians passing through the spy school.'

Kerim felt a frustrated bitterness at having so narrowly missed his target, but he tried to concentrate on the new problem.

'Have you any ideas — any suggestions as to his exact destination in Jordan, or to what he might be planning?'

'No, but I think that it must be something very important. It surprises me that he has left the villa, and I would have thought it even more unlikely that he would dare to go beyond the frontiers of Egypt. The fact that he has done so means that his business is as vital as his life itself, for Wolffe is not a brave man and he knows that if he is caught outside of Egypt then his life is immediately forfeit to the Shinbeth.'

Kerim said nothing, for suddenly his mind was running back into the old grooves, and chasing the old trails. All along he had suspected some ulterior motive behind the two hastily organized spy schools in Damascus and Jerusalem, and now the former question marks were rearing again. Only now there was a new question mark to add to the old. Mahmoud Abdel Rashid was dead, and now Otto Wolffe had left on the eve of the war for Jordan. Was Wolffe bound for Jerusalem to take Rashid's place?

Daniel's voice drew Kerim out of his thoughtful trance.

'If Wolffe is in Jordan there is nothing for you here. Will you leave, or wait for his return?'

Kerim looked up and said grimly:

'I will return to Israel.'

'How? You cannot re-cross the Sinai now that the war is raging — not even if you could find the Bedouin who brought you.'

'I have my own way out. That was part of the agreement. All that I want from you is that one of you drive me to Alexandria as soon as possible.' He paused. 'I take it that you are in radio contact with Reinhard, so you'd better warn him that Wolffe is in Jordan. And tell him that I suspect that Wolffe will reappear in Jerusalem.'

Daniel nodded. 'I think we can manage all that.' He did not say it but he was glad that Kerim had decided to leave.

* * *

There was no time to waste. It was already dawn and Daniel guessed rightly that traffic would soon come to a standstill as the exhilarant crowds swiftly filled the streets of Cairo. He personally chose to chauffeur Kerim to Alexandria and as soon as possible they went down to the car. They chose the back streets but had difficulty in getting out of the city as young Egyptians ran rampage, cheering Nasser and the wildly exaggerated war reports that crackled over Cairo radio. Heavy artillery boomed somewhere outside the city and anti-aircraft shells exploded high in the skies, although there was no sign of attacking Israeli aircraft. The mood of Cairo was one of complete jubilation and Kerim was relieved when they were clear of the crowds and could increase their speed along the open road. And he sensed that Daniel shared his feelings.

The road was fast and straight across the fertile green fields of the Nile delta, and Daniel drove the car hard. They were stopped several times where groups of eager, trigger-happy Egyptian soldiers guarded a few minor bridges, but each time their papers passed inspection. Kerim's had been forged and supplied to him by Reinhard, and were probably better than the real thing. Daniel had adopted the method of joining in the joyous high spirits that prevailed with each party of soldiers, excitedly recounting all the war bulletins that came continuously over the car radio, praising Nasser and delighting in the victorious thrashing that was supposedly being administered to Israel. In the general back-slapping and rejoicing their papers received only a nominal glance, and they were soon allowed on their way.

It was another burning hot day, and the sun was high in the brassy blue sky when they eventually reached Alexandria. Apart from the compulsory delays they had pushed on nonstop, and after three and a half hours of driving Daniel was beginning to look tired. He drove more slowly through the streets of the sea port, and they noticed that here the feeling was as high as it had been in Cairo. Cheerful crowds thronged the pavements, forming close groups around anyone who had a radio, and the atmosphere was electric with all the fever and anticipation of a successful war.

After they had eased through the crowds and the almost stationary traffic Daniel stopped the car within walking distance of the Eastern harbour. Here they parted, with no regrets and only the briefest of formal handshakes. Daniel did not even ask what Kerim's next move would be, he simply yawned and remarked that he would catch a few hours sleep at the house of a friend before making the return drive. Kerim watched the car depart with the Shinbeth man inside and was glad to be on his own. The whole trip into Egypt had been a farce and he was glad that it was over.

He walked down to the harbour and was relieved to see the *Masara*, tied up in a net-festooned huddle with a dozen or more of her sister ships. The fishing boat was deserted but he went aboard and waited, staying out of sight in the small wheelhouse.

★ ★ ★

Almost an hour passed before the joint owners of the *Masara* appeared. The two brothers were in an elated mood and had obviously been joining in the gossipy celebrations that filled the streets. They

300

clattered noisily on to the deck, still lost in a gabble of talk, and then abruptly their dark grins began to fade when they saw Kerim waiting. They were alarmed, and when he refused to leave they hustled him down into the dark and smelling hole below the wheelhouse.

Kerim sat down upon the greasy bunk where Schererzade had once lain unconscious on her stretcher, and it took him thirty minutes of persuasive argument to turn the two fishermen into a more business-like frame of mind. They were not pleased to see him, especially during the present state of affairs, but the fact that they had helped him before gave him a subtle blackmail hold, and also he was again prepared to pay heavily. Underneath his shirt he wore a fat money belt filled with American fifty dollar bills, provided by Reinhard for the purpose of ensuring his return.

Five hundred dollars in crisp cash finally overcame their reluctance, for they would almost treble that sum in Egyptian currency on the black market, and it was far more than they would earn in many a night of long arduous fishing. Omar was still doubtful, but Hakim was the elder brother with more say in their affairs, and it was he who made the decision. Kerim promised them payment as soon as the boat was at sea, for apart from the natural desire to quit Egypt as soon as possible, there was also a burning urgency inside him to return to Israel. He did not believe the bulk of the Arab news reports, but there was no doubt that the war had started, Israel was under siege, and Schererzade was trapped in Israel. There was also something else, the strange feeling of some pending revelation in his brain which he could not yet grasp, but that too was demanding his immediate return. Hakim was again uneasy about a hasty departure, preferring to wait until dusk, but on that point also he finally gave way.

That same afternoon the *Masara* cast off her mooring lines and in bright sunlight chugged quietly out into the Mediterranean.

★ ★ ★

The real crisis came a matter of six hours later. By then it was night, and with her powerful diesel engine running at full speed the *Masara* was many miles from the North African shore. Kerim had slept as well as he was able on the greasy bunk below decks, for he was tired and he knew that it was the last opportunity that he would have until the voyage was over. When he at last emerged he enjoyed the clean night air for a few minutes, and then he told the two fishermen the hard facts that he had not dared to tell them before they had sailed; namely that this time there was no waiting fishing boat from Cyprus in the open sea to the north, and that instead of making a rendezvous he wanted them to turn east and land him on the coast of Israel.

They stared at him with open disbelief on their dark faces, expressions that quickly turned to anger. For a moment there was no sound but the pulse of the engine and the swirl of the darkened sea, and then Hakim said harshly:

'This is not possible. This is not part of the bargain. If there is no boat from

Cyprus then we will take you back to Alexandria.'

Kerim said quietly, 'I am sorry, but I have to go to Israel.'

Omar, younger and always the aggressive one, snapped back hotly:

'You want to go to Israel! Arab is at war with Israel! We kill all Israel!'

He came forward and Kerim stepped back towards the bows of the boat. Kerim had hoped that this would not be necessary but now he pulled the .38 automatic from his pocket, holding it warningly. Omar saw the black glint of metal in the star-light and stopped.

Kerim repeated again, 'I am sorry. I could shoot you both and sail the *Masara* myself, but I have no wish to do that. We are old friends. Instead I will give you another five hundred dollars for the extra risk I am asking you to take. That makes one thousand dollars you will earn for a single trip.'

'You have lied to us. You have betrayed us.' Hakim's voice was still harsh. He stepped out of the wheelhouse, standing close beside his brother but with one hand still reaching back to steady the wheel. 'You allowed us to believe that there was to be another fishing boat from Cyprus. Now you want to go to Israel. The Israelies will kill us, and if not our own people will for taking you there. No, Kerim Soiron. That was not the bargain.'

'You are a spy for Israel.' Omar edged another step forward. 'A dirty, traitor spy!' His hand began to stray towards the big fisherman's knife at his hip.

Kerim said bluntly, 'Don't be foolish. Patriotism has never bothered you before. Only money counts. Don't be blinded by the national hysteria you left behind in Alexandria. Surely you must see that I cannot let you take me back. Accept the thousand dollars and be done.'

They argued, but under the threat of the gun they had no real choice. Kerim threw over his money belt and Omar dubiously counted its remaining contents note by note. The feel of the money made both of them more amenable, and at last Hakim was persuaded to change course to the east. Kerim relaxed slightly, but knew that from now on he could not dare to turn his back or close his eyes. The two fishermen were no longer his friends.

★ ★ ★

Throughout the rest of the voyage Kerim stayed in the *Masara*'s bows, out of reach and taking no chances. The two fishermen were sullen and mutinous, and not wholly resigned to their fate, and the coming of daylight made them even more nervous. It was reported that the navies of half the world were lurking in this particular sea, including the warships of the Soviet Union, Britain, Egypt, Algeria, Israel, and the American Sixth Fleet. It was not a comforting thought, and although they saw no actual ships there were several dark smudges of smoke rising from beyond the horizon that kept their nerves nicely tuned. Kerim also suffered from the broiling heat of the sun, and he experienced a great sense of relief when the day ended and the *Masara* was once again shrouded by night.

All through that second night the fishing boat ran steadily towards the coast of Israel. The seas were calm and a slight wind from behind gave an extra thrust to the throbbing engine as the bows cut through the black waves. The stars were brilliant and towards midnight the wind freshened, and shortly before dawn they saw the black line of land emerging from the dim horizon. By this time the two brothers had given up any ideas they might have had of attacking Kerim from behind. They were afraid and wanted to be rid of him so that they could hurry back to the open sea. Hakim stopped the *Masara*'s engine a mile off-shore and refused to go any closer.

He was adamant, and this time Kerim could not budge him. There was no alternative then but to go over the side and swim. It was a hostile farewell, much more so than with Daniel, and Kerim knew that he had no hope of ever being able to use the *Masara* again. If there was ever to be a next time then he would have to find another escape route out of Egypt. He turned away, stripped off his jacket, shirt and shoes, and then dived into the dark sea.

He swam quickly, half afraid that the two fishermen might grab their revenge by smashing in his bobbing head with a boat hook now that he could no longer hold them at bay. However, he need not have worried for they were too concerned over the danger of their own position to waste any time. The beat of the engine quickened almost immediately and the *Masara* heeled round in a circle and hurried swiftly away.

Kerim watched her silhouette blend into the sea and the night, and then turned and began to swim strongly towards the shore.

★ ★ ★

After five minutes he settled into a more leisurely, strength-conserving stroke. The night sky was peaceful, and although once or twice he fancied that he might have heard the very distant rumble of heavy gunfire there was nothing definite to indicate that the dark, approaching land mass ahead of him might be under assault. The sea was cold but not unpleasantly so, and initially it freshened him after the long, exhausting hours of simply staying alert and awake. His brain seemed clearer, and he swam with regular, automatic movements of his body, there was nothing to occupy his mind except thought.

His conscience was troubling him, for he could not forget the nameless little Arab girl who had been tortured in the café. Now that it was too late he was facing the fact that she would almost certainly be killed. From the point of view of Daniel and his colleagues it was the safe and logical thing to do. Daniel's appeasing words to the contrary meant nothing, and there was cowardice in allowing the Shinbeth man to turn him away.

He made an effort to shift his thinking on to a different track, and the only alternative was Otto Wolffe. Why had Wolffe left the sanctuary of Egypt to go to Jordan? And if he had gone to personally replace Rashid then what could be his purpose? The questions puzzled Kerim's brain, and once again there was the strange feeling that there was a revelation locked inside his head if only he could find the right lance of thought to trigger it into a burst of illuminating flame.

He gave it up. His body was tiring but was supported by the dark, restless waves of the sea, and his mind began to wander. To Schererzade. To Dalia. The soft, cool nights in the lemon grove. Dalia talking quietly about Rashid. There had been something out of character about Rashid. Something Dalia had told him.

And then abruptly the flame burst in his mind, flickering with doubt and disbelief, and then flaring brightly into certainty. The lethargy left him and he began to swim faster, for he believed he knew the awful thing that Wolffe intended.

19

Dangerous Streets

It was dawn when Reinhard arrived.

Kerim had emerged from the sea only half an hour before, stumbling exhausted up the sandy beach and frantically waving down the first car that had passed along the coastal road. He had been fortunate enough to stop a military jeep containing a young army officer and his driver which had swiftly conveyed him to the nearest police post. There he had put through an immediate and urgent call to Tel Aviv.

Afterwards he was kept under close guard by the armed Israeli policemen, but they gave him a towel to dry himself and found him an assortment of clothes. Their officer had talked briefly to the police department in Tel Aviv after Kerim had identified himself and asked for Reinhard, and obviously he had been told to detain his unexpected guest but to ask no questions. Hot coffee was provided and Kerim drank it thankfully while he waited. He learned from his hosts that he was roughly twenty-five miles south of Tel Aviv, and he was still finishing the last of the coffee when a car screamed noisily to a halt outside. There was a sharp exchange of voices, and then Reinhard came into the room. He had exchanged his sombre black suit for stained battle dress and a steel helmet, and there was an army revolver strapped to his hip. Behind him came a support team of two more policemen with machine pistols.

Kerim stood up to meet him, but he was not allowed the first word, and Reinhard wasted no time with formal courtesy.

'Soiron — so it is you! You are lucky that I was at headquarters when your call came through. You said that you must contact me on some vital matter that is even more important than the war itself. That had better be true. I have no time to play games.'

Kerim said bluntly, 'Did you get a report from Daniel to tell you that Otto

Wolffe is in Jordan?'

'Yes, we received a radio message to that effect.'

'Did the message also add my belief that Wolffe may be in Jerusalem.'

'It did, but I considered your opinion unlikely.' Reinhard's mouth was snapping like a steel trap, and the light was flashing from his square-rimmed glasses. 'You may not be aware of the fact but a war has been raging for the past two days. We have smashed the Egyptians and have hurled them back across the Sinai, and on the Jordanian front our troops are even now launching the last battle for Jerusalem. There has been heavy fighting, and only our fear of damaging the Holy churches has delayed our capture of the old city. Wolffe would not risk his neck where the blood is being spilled.'

'You're wrong!' Kerim contradicted flatly. 'Wolffe went to Jerusalem to carry out the job he had previously given to Rashid. I believed all along that there was something more than ordinary sabotage behind those two spy schools that Rashid organized, and now I think I know what the real targets are. I've already told you about Dalia, the girl who was killed in the lemon grove. She mentioned to me once that Rashid had an interest in the Holy churches of Jerusalem, he even had plans and drawings of the Holy Sepulchre locked in his desk. Wolffe intends to destroy the Tomb of Christ and the other Sacred Relics of your religion. The very places that you are so afraid of causing harm!'

There was a shocked and agonized silence. The commander of the police post and the half dozen of his men who crowded the room stared uncertainly at Kerim's face. Then Reinhard said slowly:

'Wolffe would not risk his own life. He does not have that kind of courage.'

'What life?' Kerim demanded scornfully. 'His life is almost at an end. He's an old man — an old, persecuted man with a pathological hatred for Israel and the Jews. There's nothing left in him but loathing and fear. He wants to strike a final, lasting blow of revenge against you and all your kind, and what more effective blow could he strike than by destroying the very things you hold more dear than life itself.'

Reinhard looked worried now, he hesitated and then said:

'You forget that in many cases the places held sacred by our religion are also Holy to the Arabs. Islam believes that Christ was an important prophet, even though they do not accept that he was The Son of God. Also the Arabs would not risk the possibility of Israeli retaliation against their own spiritual centre in Jerusalem, the Dome Of The Rock. The Dome is a sanctuary second in importance only to Mecca in the Islamic faith. Wolffe's Arab masters would not dare to allow the deed you suggest.'

'But Wolffe is not acting with the knowledge of his Arab masters.' Kerim explained it patiently. 'Wolffe is obeying only his hatred for the Jews.'

Reinhard licked his lips, and suddenly he did not seem to know what to do with his long, sinewy hands. He had stopped arguing now and had accepted that the possibility was real.

'If you are right, then Wolffe will wait until the last minute to put his plans into effect. He will strike in the final confusion while the old city is beyond the control of either Arabs or Jews.' He glanced at his watch. 'The final assault was opened upon Jerusalem at dawn this morning. The Jordanians have already been cleared from the surrounding hills, but we will have to take the city street by street. There may yet be time.'

He turned to snap a string of words in Hebrew to the commander of the police post. The officer nodded anxiously and turned swiftly towards the telephone. Reinhard's two aides had anticipated their orders and were hurrying out of the room, and without waiting to be invited Kerim joined Reinhard as he followed. They ran down the sandbag-lined steps to where a large black car waited at the kerb and quickly scrambled inside. Reinhard himself took the wheel and in a matter of seconds they were driving fast towards the Jordanian battlefront and the beleagured city of Jerusalem. The dawn had advanced and the sky was a pale blue grey.

★ ★ ★

Reinhard drove like a man possessed, skidding and swerving and hurling up clouds of dust from their tyres as he passed every other vehicle on the road. The powerful car never slowed below ninety miles per hour, and Reinhard's concentration was complete. He did not speak once. As they neared the frontier with Jordan Kerim saw ugly black smoke clouds dirtying the skyline, and blotting out the low sun. Repeatedly they now heard the recoiling thunder of tanks and artillery, and once a trio of French-built Mystre jet fighters howled overhead, flashing the Star of David on their wings. One of Reinhard's two aides, and Kerim had realized by now that these were also Shinbeth men, tersely confided that the Israeli pilots were in complete command of the skies. They had destroyed the numerically superior Arab air forces during the first day of

317

the war, and more recently they had been busy in saturating the Jordanian strongholds around Jerusalem with shells, rockets and napalm.

Reinhard was forced to slow as they entered the Israeli side of Jerusalem under the pall of thinning smoke. Stray shells were still falling, windows were smashed, buildings demolished, and tanks and armour still lumbered through streets littered with craters and burned-out cars. Tough Israeli troops in leopard-patterned battle dress poured steadily along the pavements, their dirt-smudged faces alert but jubilant under the hard rims of their steel helmets, rifles, machine pistols, bren guns and bazookas cradled in their hands. Then their car was stopped by a young platoon commander with a dozen soldiers behind him and a machine gun in his hands. Reinhard talked to him swiftly in Hebrew and then the man was shouting orders to scatter his men out of their path, at the same time swinging on to the running board of the car to act as their guide.

The car twisted through the smoke-shrouded streets, avoiding the worst of the craters, and Kerim realized that they were heading towards the Mandelbaum gate. The area here had been very badly hit indeed, pounded by shells and bazooka fire and they had difficulty in getting through. Finally they lurched to a stop before a forward police post where an ironfaced Sergeant and a squad of soldiers forced them to a halt.

The police post had been turned into a battle headquarters and inside they found a Colonel, two Majors, and a Captain working like beavers among a small group of orderlies around three field telephones and a table scattered with maps. An urgent conference followed. The Army officers were at first incredulous but Reinhard's credentials earned him the benefit of the doubt. Then things moved fast. To Kerim it was all confusion, but hurried telephone calls were made and within ten minutes two armoured cars filled with more steel-helmeted troops rolled to a stop before the command post. One of the Shinbeth men found a spare helmet and cheerfully jammed it upon Kerim's head. On impulse Kerim asked for a weapon and was swiftly provided with a brand new machine pistol of Czech origin, one of the many captured from the enemy.

They went out to the armoured cars, and another rushed conference with the young Lieutenant in charge of the two vehicles. Many of these Israeli officers seemed to be very young, but they grasped facts swiftly. The Lieutenant looked no more than twenty, and his name was Bernard.

Within a very few minutes they were moving off again towards the Mandelbaum Gate. Kerim rode in the first armoured car between Reinhard and Bernard, together with one of the Majors from the command post who had come to lend the weight of authority, and as many of the armed soldiers as could cram themselves into the back. Reinhard's two aides followed in the second car which was again over-flowing with soldiers, and bristling with automatic rifles and machine guns.

Exasperated, Kerim said:

'Reinhard, for Christ's sake tell me what's going on. I don't understand all your blasted Hebrew.'

Reinhard favoured him with a few terse words in English.

'It is simple. Jerusalem is almost taken and there is not much time to waste. Two armoured columns of Israeli troops have encircled the city in a classic pincer movement, and now the pincers are being closed. Even at this very moment our advance forces are probably penetrating into the old city itself, but now the fighting is bloody and is mostly being done with knives to prevent damage to the Holy places. Radio warnings have been sent to all forward troop and tank commanders to be alert for Wolffe and his agents, but they have a war to fight, and so it is our task to stop Wolffe. Major Levin has come with us to clear the way through our own forces, and also because he has had previous experience with bomb disposal. His talents may be needed.'

The Major smiled somewhat bleakly,

but he was an older, silent man who made no comment.

They were now passing through the heavily savaged area of the Mandelbaum Gate, entering what had been Jordanian Jerusalem. Their driver had to manoeuvre past the gutted shells of burned-out tanks and cars, more gaping craters in the roadway, and more horribly the scattered corpses of Jordan's Arab soldiers. The sound of rifle and machine gun fire still rattled through the swirls of smoke that lay in the streets, and it was obvious that there were still many isolated pockets of Arab resistance to be cleaned out.

They passed an overturned Land Rover with an Arab soldier hanging dead from the front seat, his arms and forehead touching the dirt as though in a last supplication to Allah. Some of his comrades lay nearby, dead beside their fallen arms, huddled and sightless, mouths still open in the agony of dying. For them the holy war had betrayed its promises. Buildings reflected the savage accuracy of young Israeli pilots and some still burned. The armoured cars lurched on and then abruptly a machine gun opened up from a window high above. Bullets sprayed in a hideous ricocheting whine from the steel bonnet of the lead car, and then an answering hail flew up from the alert soldiers squashed into the back and the single gun from the window was silenced. Other lurking snipers risked single rifle shots, but there was no time to answer them effectively.

Kerim had flinched when the car had been hit. He said flatly:

'Pretty warm, isn't it?'

Major Levin smiled wearily and surprised him by speaking.

'Not really, after the past two days it is comparatively peaceful. Two nights ago the sky above Jerusalem was crimson, it seemed as though the whole city had been blotted out by smoke and fire. Now it is over. There are only the snipers left.'

Kerim glanced at him and realized that Levin was tired, the Major was hollow-eyed and probably had not slept since the war started. The young Lieutenant Bernard looked the same, so did Reinhard, and even the troops behind them. They were all battle-weary, and it was not surprising that they were non-communicative. It reminded him that he too had not slept for the best part of two days.

The armoured cars sped on through the dangerous streets. Both drivers knew the urgency of their mission and took nerve-wracking risks, overtaking other Israeli units as they rushed past the great walls that encircled the old city. Arab snipers were crouched above the walls and in the upper rooms of many of the surrounding buildings, while tough Israeli para-troopers sought to knock them out with blazing guns. They not only had to take the city street by street, but house by house. The two cars ignored the conflict and the outbreaks of hostile bullets, and finally swung through the St Stephen's Gate into the heart of the old city. The gate was firmly in Israeli hands and the presence of Major Levin allowed them to speed straight through.

They hurried down the Via Dolorosa,

The Way Of The Cross, where Christ had walked nearly two thousand years ago, with a crown of thorns upon his head and the sins of the world upon his shoulders. Now it was lined with eucalyptus trees, and ugly barriers of barbed wire. There was still fierce fighting in the narrow streets on either side, but the struggle was more silent. Here Arabs and Jews fought with knives, willing to kill each other, but not to damage the sacred city of their religions.

If Kerim was right only one man wanted that.

Otto Wolffe.

The two armoured cars stopped as close as possible to the site of the Holy Sepulchre; the huge grey-domed church, its construction half Byzantine and half Crusader, which was built over the scenes of the crucifixion, burial and resurrection of Jesus Christ, and was now the shrine of the Christian world. The troops scrambled quickly down into the dusty street, gripping their weapons, and their Lieutenant gave swift orders to move forward and seal off all entrances to the church. They obeyed fast and nobody stayed behind. Kerim accompanied Reinhard and the Major.

20

The Black Wolf

The Holy Sepulchre was set in a warren of twisting, ancient streets, and surrounded by a throng of smaller chapels and monasteries of different denominations. Now all the tiny shops were shuttered and the streets were empty. A few frantic Arabs scattered like flapping ghosts before them, but not a shot was fired as the grim-faced Israeli troops filtered through the maze to take up their positions. Bernard led a party of his men to the right to circle behind the church, while the two Shinbeth men went with the grizzled old Sergeant who had commanded the second armoured car, their party fanning out to the left. Kerim, Reinhard and Levin made directly for the main entrance into the church.

It was a vast, old building, and seemingly supported by the cluttering embraces of rickety wooden scaffolding. Inside there were piles of sand, uprooted flagstones, and a scattering of tools and wheelbarrows. Reinhard commented that restoration work had been in progress before the advent of the war, but despite the disparaging traces of the workmen his voice was low and reverent. The great, towering central dome was still a noble sight, and the small, enclosed chapels built above Calvary, the Burial Cave, and the Tomb Of Christ, all reflected their own quiet beauty. There were quite a number of people in evidence, mostly women and children seeking refuge from the ugly violence outside, mixed with a mingling of black-robed monks and priests, Greek Orthodox, Catholic, Armenian and others. Many of the visitors knelt and prayed.

The three men found a reluctance to penetrate too deeply inside the church. Reinhard and Levin wore holstered revolvers, and Kerim had self-consciously slung his borrowed machine pistol over his shoulder out of the way. Weapons were out of place in here. They looked

328

all around them, and then Reinhard said softly:

'Nothing has happened yet, that much is obvious. And for all practical purposes Jerusalem is in Israeli hands. You could have been wrong.'

Doubt was in his voice again. They had won the race, but now he would look foolish if there was no race at all.

'Better safe than sorry,' Kerim said weakly. The cliché sounded inane and he too was suffering the first pangs of doubt. There had been no time to think during their frantic haste to get here, but now the whole idea was beginning to seem impossible. He had convinced himself and convinced Reinhard, but apart from the drawings that Dalia had seen in Rashid's desk there was no real proof.

On the far side of the church they saw Bernard. The young Lieutenant had appeared with two of his soldiers behind him, three hesitant men in leopard-patterned uniforms, embarrassed by their weapons and not sure what to do next. Reinhard raised his hand in a stopping

329

gesture that made them stand still.

They were attracting attention now. Reinhard and Levin also wore battle dress, and all of them wore steel helmets. They could not escape the stares as their presence was noted. A few of the watching faces showed alarm, but most were relieved that it was not the Arab Legion of Jordan who had invaded the precincts of the church. Some faces were frankly joyful. A deputation of priests began to move towards them.

Kerim was searching for faces he knew, faces from the spy school, or the photograph face of Otto Wolffe, but the faces were all innocent strangers.

Levin took control, authority in his voice.

'Spread out. Take a look at all the chapels. If there is any kind of a bomb it will probably look harmless, a paper parcel, a carrier bag, something similar. Anything you find, call me immediately. I'll have a word with the priests — get them searching too. Be less panic that way than filling the church with soldiers.'

The Major was already moving away

to meet the approaching deputation. Reinhard said briefly:

'I'll take the Tomb — check the Calvary chapel.'

Kerim nodded. Reinhard left him and hurried towards the small but ornate chapel that contained the Tomb Of Christ, the Holy of Holies in this centre of long centuries of devotion. Kerim turned towards the Calvary chapel, passing close to some kneeling Jews, businessmen or shop-owners, who watched him uncertainly. He knew he cut a strange figure in ill-fitting, borrowed trousers, a police uniform jacket and steel helmet, but he was not here to win a beauty competition. He stopped before the steep steps leading up to the mound of Calvary with its commemorating shrine, and he was still alert for faces rather than suspicious looking parcels.

He started up the steps. Jesus Christ had been crucified on this tiny hill, now enclosed by the overall vastness of the huge church, and he could sense the prayers it had inspired throughout the ages. Despite the urgency he hesitated.

He was reluctant to take his machine pistol inside. Perhaps he should leave it on the steps.

From one side he saw a tall man in a brown habit bound with rope striding determinedly towards him. A Franciscan monk, one of the chapel guardians. Beyond the monk another man moved, shabby, ordinary clothes, jacket and trousers, a dark face, hurrying through the shadows behind the great columns that supported the high roof. The dark, half-seen face stabbed in Kerim's memory and he wheeled on the steps, startling the monk as he rushed down again.

The man passing behind the columns saw him and fled.

'Stop that man!'

Kerim's shout electrified the uncertain atmosphere in the church, ringing in noisy echoes beneath the high dome. The anxious monk got in his way as he dived after the fugitive and he had to brush the restraining figure in the brown habit aside. Cries of protest and alarm created sudden pandemonium as the running fugitive headed directly for the exit.

Reinhard appeared at a run, clawing his revolver from its holster but reluctant to loose a shot. Levin was still surrounded by the small group of priests who were listening closely but dubiously to his explanations, and he too was delayed in getting through them. Bernard was running hard from the far side of the church but he was much too far away.

Kerim scrambled over an intervening pile of sand, the machine pistol now gripped in his hands. The columns were in his way but even so he still would not have violated the interior of the church with gunfire. He sprinted through the line of columns and chased the dark-skinned fugitive towards the exit. No one appeared to block him off and the man vanished. Kerim almost collided with Reinard as they passed through the open doors in pursuit.

The fugitive was racing down the road ahead of them. A whistle shrilled in a clear sharp blast, and the Israeli Sergeant and one of Reinhard's Shinbeth aides appeared to cut off his escape. The fugitive twisted and tried another turning, but realized in the same moment that he was trapped on all sides as the waiting soldiers closed in. Reinhard shouted an order to stop and the man did so, turning in the centre of the road, screaming abuse and drawing a revolver.

Kerim flung himself into a doorway, lifting the machine pistol. He didn't have to use it for Reinhard had already taken swift aim. They were outside the church now and he didn't hesitate to shoot. The bark of the gun heralded a screech of agony as their quarry dropped his own weapon and toppled forward on to his face, his hands grabbing at his shattered kneecap.

One of the soldiers reached him first, and then Kerim and Reinhard ran to join him. The fugitive still writhed and moaned on the ground with blood staining the cloth of his trouser leg.

Kerim said grimly:

'He was one of the students from the convent. I recognized him as he was trying to slip away.'

There was a clatter of boots as the Sergeant and the Shinbeth man ran up. Reinhard said briskly:

'Get your men back to their positions, Sergeant. Don't let anyone else pass through the cordon.'

The Sergeant nodded, grasping the situation without asking any questions. He and his men melted back into the surrounding streets. Only the Shinbeth man stayed.

Reinhard knelt by the injured man in the road, heaving him into a sitting position against the wall. He gripped the man's hair, yanked his head back and thrust a levelled revolver before his eyes. His body was almost trembling as he said viciously:

'Listen closely, you whoring son of a camel. I want to know where you placed the explosives in the church? And I want to know where to find the rest of your friends from that stupid spy school? And especially where to find Otto Wolffe?'

The Arab made a sobbing noise and tried to indicate his bullet-smashed knee. Reinhard swiped him across the face with the barrel of the revolver and then jabbed the still-warm muzzle against the squirming throat.

'Answer me! Or by God I'll blast your teeth through the top of your thick Arab skull!'

The man still sobbed and wriggled helplessly, but he was saved by the sudden arrival of Bernard. The young Lieutenant ran up beside them and said breathlessly:

'We've got another of his friends. My men stopped him as he tried to slip past on the other side of the church. And we've found two bombs. One was a carpenter's bag filled with plastic explosive and a crude time clock. It had been left just outside the Tomb of Christ, close against the wall. There was a similar bag beside the Calvary chapel. There was enough explosives in them to blow both places to pieces, but Major Levin is now taking care of them. The tool bags were an ideal cover with the church undergoing restoration. The two Arabs walked in pretending to be workmen.'

Kerim said thankfully, 'It's fortunate

that some of us got our priorities right and stayed behind, but are you sure you've got the lot?'

'Pretty sure, sir.' The younger man sounded positive. 'Major Levin has got everything under control, and now that the priests are alive to the danger they are carrying out a more thorough search.'

Reinhard's face was still bleak, a cavernous grey funeral mask behind the squared glasses.

'Is there any sign of Wolffe?'

'None, sir. There's nobody inside the church who remotely fits that description.'

Reinhard hesitated, and then turned back to the pathetic wretch that was their prisoner. Three minutes of hard interrogation sufficed to tell them that although Wolffe was definitely in Jerusalem the man honestly did not know where the German was now.

Bernard said tentatively, 'There are other targets. The Tomb Of David outside the city, or the Wailing Wall?'

Reinhard shook his head. 'No, the Holy Sepulchre would be the main target. If Wolffe is doing any of his own dirty work then he would be here. We may catch some more of the students from his spy school at the other places, but not Wolffe himself.'

Kerim had been thinking hard. He said slowly:

'There is one other possibility. One target that Wolffe could not possibly delegate to any of his students. One that he would have to tackle personally, even without their knowledge. The Dome Of The Rock.'

Reinhard stared at him. 'But the Dome is only sacred to Islam. Why should Wolffe betray his friends?'

Certainty was hardening once more in Kerim's mind.

'Can't you see? Wolffe is doing all this without the knowledge of his Arab friends, although his students will not be aware of that. If those home-made bombs had damaged the Holy Sepulchre, and then shortly afterwards a similar outrage occurs at the Dome, then the Arabs will be convinced that it is Israeli retaliation. Your people will be blamed for what happens at the Dome. The Arabs will never forgive you — and if you had not found out the truth in time, would you have forgiven them for destroying the Tomb of Christ? If Wolffe has his way there will never be peace between the Arabs and Jews, there will be bloodshed for evermore. That is Wolffe's vengeance. This war is almost over, but he wants to be sure that there will be others. He wants the present hatred and fanaticism kept up to the same burning pitch where the complete annihilation of the whole Jewish race is the only Arab aim. Wolffe wants the Arabs to finish what the Nazis started.'

Kerim finished speaking and found that his throat was hoarse. Bernard was staring at him and the young Lieutenant's face was frankly horrified. Reinhard was again convinced and even he looked shaken. He turned quickly to the waiting Shinbeth man by his side.

'Quickly, warn Major Levin of what is happening. Ask him to follow us as soon as he has dismantled the bombs inside the church. We are going to the Dome Of The Rock.' The Shinbeth man left at a run but Reinhard's words still tumbled out. 'Lieutenant, leave a man to guard this pig of an Arab. Bring the rest of your men with me.'

Bernard obeyed smartly, yelling orders. His Sergeant appeared with half a dozen soldiers, but they could not afford to wait for more. Reinhard was already moving off at a run with Kerim at his heels. Bernard followed with his soldiers, while one reluctant Israeli private stayed to point an automatic rifle at the cringing head of the wounded prisoner.

They ran at full pelt through the maze of narrow, biblical streets. Normally the bazaars would be full of life and bustle but now they were empty and the shops shuttered. Faint crackles of gunfire were all around them but none were close. Reinhard faltered at a choice of three roads, but Kerim knew the area well and forged past him to take the lead, turning left and plunging down shallow steps through an old stone archway. Behind him the road led back to the Petra Hotel where he had stayed on his last visit, ahead the road continued to the Moslem sanctuary.

They rushed through more ancient archways, and finally tumbled breathlessly through the great open gateway to the Haram-Es-Sharif, the Arab name for the Noble Sanctuary. To their right was the Wailing Wall, the only remaining part of the Temple of Herod where Jews had lamented their sorrows for centuries past. Already a few early units of Israeli troops were praying there and kissing the time-worn stones. Also to their right was the vast Al-Aqsa Mosque where five thousand Moslems could kneel at any one time to pray, while directly ahead lay the great platform of Herod that now supported the magnificent, octagonal shaped Dome Of The Rock, the sunshine gleaming on the great golden pearl of the dome. The rest of the walled sanctuary was made up of smaller domed shrines, and quiet courtyards shaded by dark green trees.

They hesitated only a moment, and then hurried directly to the great octagonal mosque. Kerim and Reinhard were side by side once more as they went up the smooth steps to the giant platform base.

Bernard was only a step behind and already ordering his handful of men to spread out. There was no one to resist them and within a matter of minutes they reached the closed bronze doors. There was a moment of indecision, and then Reinhard rapped an order. Bernard stepped past him and used his machine pistol to shoot the lock off. All three of them pushed inside.

They were in one of the most beautiful buildings in the world. Before them a low wooden railing enclosed a central area of bare, virgin rock, the site from which the Prophet Mohammed had ascended to paradise. The carpets around the central area were a deep, plush red, and there was no part of the eight interior walls and ceiling that was not gorgeously decorated with blue and gold, mosaic, stained glass, and flowing text from the Koran. It was a splendid, breath-catching monument, glowing, and even more inspiring of reverence than the Holy Sepulchre had been.

The three men stood still, sharply conscious of what they had done in shooting the lock from the door, afraid and regretting the act. Here was much of the past history of Islam. As well as being the site of the ascension the rock was also venerated by the faithful as the place where their common ancestor Abraham made ready to sacrifice his son to God, and later it had been the altar of the temple of Solomon, the son of David. Like the Holy Sepulchre it had seen centuries of devotion.

At the moment it appeared to be empty. Kerim was uncertain, Bernard unashamedly hung back, and only Reinhard moved to circle round the mosque. Then abruptly there came the sound of shouts and a disturbance from outside. The three men exchanged glances and then hurried back into the blinding sunlight.

A spate of gunfire and shouted commands ordering some unseen party to stop led them in a frantic scramble round to the back of the building. Bernard's Sergeant was doing the shouting and the rest of the soldiers were converging swiftly upon the spot. Kerim noticed a rope dangling down from the roof of the mosque and a man running clumsily away. The man was old and slow, and hampered by a heavy pack strapped to his shoulders. His hair was grey and there was no doubting his identity.

They had found Otto Wolffe.

The German was running down from the great platform and heading into the dusty gardens. The troops were close, shouting and yelling but holding their fire, like schoolboys in a chase that they knew they had won. Then Wolffe turned and they all saw the automatic in his hand. He fired once and the pursuing Sergeant was suddenly spinning round and falling. The soldiers changed expression, stopping in their tracks and levelling their own weapons. Reinhard howled at the top of his voice:

'I want him alive!'

There was a pause, fractional confusion. Wolffe took his opportunity to fire another shot and then continue his flight, dodging behind a small white-domed shrine. Kerim had slowed but Reinhard bounded past him, his face contorted with unholy vigour.

'Take him alive! *I want him alive!*'

Bernard followed him and the soldiers rallied once more, spreading out like a team of beaters flushing game. Wolffe had the edge now that they would not shoot to kill, but they were still determined.

Kerim stopped for a moment by the wounded Sergeant. The man had rolled on to his side and now supported himself on one elbow, pressing his right hand against the red patch over his ribs. He said tightly:

'He was trying to climb on to the roof, sir — half-way up the rope when I saw him. He dropped down when I shouted and then ran for it.' He coughed and finished. 'I'm okay, sir. Been expecting this for two days.'

Kerim nodded and then ran on, down the steps from the platform and chasing across a dusty courtyard to rejoin Reinhard. Wolffe was cornered now, trapped against the far wall of the sanctuary with the Israelies closing in around him. The German stood upright to face his enemies, hate and fear and pathos written into the worn lines of his face. An old man with nowhere left to run. He shot one of the approaching soldiers dead and wounded another, forcing the remainder to take cover.

Reinhard crouched behind a low wall, still shouting.

'Aim for his legs! Cut him down but take him alive!'

The soldiers obeyed, opening fire thankfully but firing low. Wolffe chose that same moment to drop down on to one knee in order to make himself into a smaller target, and one of the fusillade of bullets struck the large pack that was still fastened to his shoulders.

The result was a terrifying blast of fire and deafening sound. Its effects felled a slender cypress tree and demolished another of the small white domes into a pile of rubble. The nearest of the attacking soldiers were hurled off their feet like dummies caught in a swirl of wind and the air was filled with smoke and flying dirt and stones. The effect on Otto Wolffe was even more drastic for the luckless German was literally blown to pieces, adding shreds of blood and flesh and bone to the general mess.

A chunk of whirling brick had cracked into Kerim's steel helmet, toppling him down and rendering him dizzy. When he straightened up a deep hush had settled upon the scene, the troops were picking themselves up and staring and one or two looked a sickly grey. Reinhard had the face of a man who had been robbed and beaten in the moment of his triumph, one side of his glasses was cracked and he did not want to believe what he saw. Then Bernard said faintly:

'Oh God. Holy Mother of God. What happened?'

Kerim had not realized that the young Lieutenant was so close beside him. He turned and saw that the boy's face was stark white. His own stomach felt weak but he managed to answer.

'The pack must have been stuffed full of explosives. If he had got on to the roof of the mosque he would have planted them close against the dome.'

Reinhard was only a few yards in front of them, but the Shinbeth man was not listening. He said bitterly:

'I wanted him alive. Not dead. *Alive!*'

He went forward like a man in a trance, still holding the revolver he had not dared to use, searching vaguely around the scene of the explosion. No one else moved.

It was then that Kerim saw the grisly object that had landed in the grass close to his feet. He swallowed his revulsion and gingerly picked it up, holding the thumb as though it were the tail of a dead rat. He walked after Reinhard and said quietly:

'Is this what you want?'

Reinhard stared at him through his cracked glasses, barely noticing the severed hand with the zig-zag scar still clearly visible across the back of the fingers. There were tears in his eyes and a note of bitter fury in his voice.

'I wanted him alive,' he repeated. 'Can't you understand — I wanted him alive.'

Kerim hesitated, and then dropped the dead man's hand at his feet. He turned away and left Reinhard to cry his impotent tears of frustration, but for himself there was no emotion left at all. The sun was shining, Jerusalem was taken, and the Black Wolf was dead. But the tears and the elation were for others, Kerim could only feel a terrible, aching weariness.

21

Sanctuary

The date was the tenth of June. The short but savage six day war was over, with the Arab armies soundly thrashed and Israeli frontiers extended on all sides. The Egyptians had been humiliatingly crushed in the Sinai, and the triumphant Israeli tank columns had not halted their steamrollering charge until they had reached the very banks of the Suez Canal. The blockade of the Gulf of Aqaba had been lifted. The Jordanian front had collapsed back to the Jordan River, and in Syria the Israeli troops were poised on the road to Damascus. The military victory was complete, and now there was nothing left but to count the hideous toll of death and destruction and the pathetic refugees that the war had left in its wake.

In Tel Aviv Kerim was reunited

with Schererzade, but he could not immediately take her into his arms and kiss her as he so dearly wanted. Reinhard's presence prevented that. The Shinbeth man had kept his promise to release the girl now that Otto Wolffe was dead, and had accompanied Kerim to the hotel where she was being detained. So there was some uncertainty and embarrassment, and Reinhard was not sensitive enough to realize that he was the cause.

In the awkward silence that fell after the first few minutes of their meeting Reinhard said:

'Well, Soiron, what will you do now? You are both free, but I hardly think that you can return to your old employer, Major Jackson.'

Kerim looked at him warily. Reinhard was once again wearing his funeral black suit, and his long face was strangely disquieting behind the cracked glasses. Kerim sensed that there was something behind the question. He replied obliquely:

'I knew that.'

Reinhard nodded wisely, and then said directly:

'There is a place for you in the Shinbeth. I could use your talents.'

'No.' The refusal was positive. 'I am finished with all that. You and Jackson, and all the rest of your kind, can play your stupid, dirty little games without any help from me. I don't have enough greed, or hate, or conceit, not anymore.'

Reinhard gave him a peculiar look, but he showed no malice. Schererzade was seated in an armchair close by Kerim's side, looking beautiful but nervous in a pale blue dress that left her brown arms bare, and he turned his attention to her.

'And you? I can find you a place in Damascus or Amman. You will do the same kind of work for me as you did for — '

'No.' Again it was Kerim who spoke, and again he was positive. His hand closed over her shoulder as she looked up startled at his face, but he was still gazing at Reinhard. He said flatly:

'Schererzade and I are to be married.'

The assumption was a bold one, but after a moment he felt her hand covering his own where he gripped her shoulder, pressing gently. He dared to look down then and a smile of approval was trembling on her lips.

'I see.'

Reinhard sounded as though he didn't fully see at all, but the Shinbeth man was dwindling into insignificance. Kerim Soiron was filled with a new power that made him ten feet tall, and he was making all the decisions now.

'There is just one favour that you can do for us,' he said. 'But this time with no strings or conditions. I think you owe us just one favour without a price.'

Reinhard regarded them gravely.

'Perhaps. If your request is reasonable and possible, then I will try to help.'

* * *

A few days later Kerim and Schererzade arrived at a kibbutz, one of the communal farming settlements of Israel where they were to live and work. Their request for asylum had been influenced by Reinhard, and despite the condition that they were now enlisted as soldiers in the Israel Army Reserve they were both satisfied. That one condition applied to every settler in Israel and they had not expected to be immune, and at least in the next war they would be fighting openly and honourably on the battlefield.

The kibbutz was a village of flat-roofed, white-washed houses, a communal dining hall, milking sheds and cow barns; all clean and simple, and enclosed by vegetable plots, vineyards, and date palms. It offered hot sunshine, outdoor living, cheerful companions and hard work.

Kerim picked up a handful of soil and let it trickle through his fingers. At least it was clean dirt. Schererzade was beside him, her waist fitting warmly into the tight circle of his arm, and they had no regrets.

A LANCE FOR THE DEVIL
Robert Charles

The funeral service of Pope Paul VI was to be held in the great plaza before St. Peter's Cathedral in Rome, and was to be the scene of the most monstrous mass assassination of political leaders the world had ever known. Only Counter-Terror could prevent it.

IN THAT RICH EARTH
Alan Sewart

How long does it take for a human body to decay until only the bones remain? When Detective Sergeant Harry Chamberlane received news of a body, he raised exactly that question. But whose was the body? Who was to blame for the death and in what circumstances?

MURDER AS USUAL
Hugh Pentecost
A psychotic girl shot and killed Mac Crenshaw, who had come to the New England town with the advance party for Senator Farraday. Private detective David Cotter agreed that the girl was probably just a pawn in a complex game — but who had sent her on the assignment?

THE MARGIN
Ian Stuart
It is rumoured that Walkers Brewery has been selling arms to the South African army, and Graham Lorimer is asked to investigate. He meets the beautiful Shelley van Rynveld, who is dedicated to ending apartheid. When a Walkers employee is killed in a hit-and-run accident, his wife tells Graham that he's been seeing Shelly van Rynveld . . .

TOO LATE FOR THE FUNERAL
Roger Ormerod

Carol Turner, seventeen, and a mystery, is very close to a murder, and she has in her possession a weapon that could prove a number of things. But it is Elsa Mallin who suffers most before the truth of Carol Turner releases her.

NIGHT OF THE FAIR
Jay Baker

The gun was the last of the things for which Harry Judd had fought and now it was in the hands of his worst enemy, aimed at the boy he had tried to help. This was the night in which the past had to be faced again and finally understood.

MR CRUMBLESTONE'S EDEN

Henry Crumblestone was a quiet little man who would never knowingly have harmed another, and it was a dreadful twist of irony that caused him to kill in defence of a dream . . .

PAY-OFF IN SWITZERLAND
Bill Knox

'Hot' British currency was being smuggled to Switzerland to be laundered, hidden in a safari-style convoy heading across Europe. Jonathan Gaunt, external auditor for the Queen's and Lord Treasurer's Remembrancer, went along with the safari, posing as a tourist, to get any lead he could. But sudden death trailed the convoy every kilometer to Lake Geneva.

SALVAGE JOB
Bill Knox

A storm has left the oil tanker S.S. *Craig Michael* stranded and almost blocking the only channel to the bay at Cabo Esco. Sent to investigate, marine insurance inspector Laird discovers that the Portuguese bay is hiding a powder keg of international proportions.

BOMB SCARE — FLIGHT 147
Peter Chambers

Smog delayed Flight 147, and so prevented a bomb exploding in mid-air. Walter Keane found that during the crisis he had been robbed of his jewel bag, and Mark Preston was hired to locate it without involving the police. When a murder was committed, Preston knew the stake had grown.

STAMBOUL INTRIGUE
Robert Charles

Greece and Turkey were on the brink of war, and the conflict could spell the beginning of the end for the Western defence pact of N.A.T.O. When the rumour of a plot to speed this possibility reached Counter-espionage in Whitehall, Simon Larren and Adrian Cleyton were despatched to Turkey . . .

CRACK IN THE SIDEWALK
Basil Copper

After brilliant scientist Professor Hopcroft is knocked down and killed by a car, L.A. private investigator Mike Faraday discovers that his death was murder and that differing groups are engaged in a power struggle for The Zetland Method. As Mike tries to discover what The Zetland Method is, corpses and hair-breadth escapes come thick and fast . . .

DEATH OF A MACHINE
Charles Leader

When Mike M'Call found the mutilated corpse of a marine in an alleyway in Singapore, a thousand-strong marine battalion was hell-bent on revenge for their murdered comrade — and the next target for the tong gang of paid killers appeared to be M'Call himself . . .

ANYONE CAN MURDER
Freda Bream

Hubert Carson, the editorial Manager of the Herald Newspaper in Auckland, is found dead in his office. Carson's fellow employees knew that the unpopular chief reporter, Clive Yarwood, wanted Carson's job — but did he want it badly enough to kill for it?

CART BEFORE THE HEARSE
Roger Ormerod

Sometimes a case comes up backwards. When Ernest Connelly said 'I have killed . . .', he did not name the victim. So Dave Mallin and George Coe find themselves attempting to discover a body to fit the crime.

SALESMAN OF DEATH
Charles Leader

For Mike M'Call, selling guns in Detroit proves a dangerous business — from the moment of his arrival in the middle of a racial plot, to the final clash of arms between two rival groups of militant extremists.

THE FOURTH SHADOW
Robert Charles

Simon Larren merely had to ensure that the visiting President of Maraquilla remained alive during a goodwill tour of the British Crown Colony of San Quito. But there were complications. Finally, there was a Communist-inspired bid for illegal independence from British rule, backed by the evil of voodoo.

SCAVENGERS AT WAR
Charles Leader

Colonel Piet Van Velsen needed an experienced officer for his mercenary commando, and Mike M'Call became a reluctant soldier. The Latin American Republic was torn apart by revolutionary guerrilla groups — but why were the ruthless Congo veterans unleashed on a province where no guerrilla threat existed?